Reading Between the Lives

by

Ashantay Peters

Reading Between the Lives

Cover Art by *Diana Carlile*

The Wild Rose Press, Inc.
PO Box 708
Adams Basin, NY 14410-0708
Visit us at www.thewildrosepress.com

Publishing History
First Fantasy Rose Edition, 2016
Print ISBN 978-1-5092-0859-3
Digital ISBN 978-1-5092-0860-9

Published in the United States of America

"You know, if I had a beautiful, sexy woman like yours, I'd treat her the way she deserved rather than embarrassing her by coming on to the server in front of her. Or even behind her back."

His brown gaze entangled mine. "No offense, sweets, but you look too intelligent to stick yourself with low-rent goods."

I don't know if I'd have responded even if the royal blue light emanating from around his hands and head hadn't caught my eye. My elbow rested on the table with my chin in my hand for a better look in a fluid motion I hadn't known I could execute.

In what seemed a totally natural move, my gaze traveled from the light phenomenon to Mr. Calendar's eyes. If I thought I'd been hypnotized by the blue marvel, I wasn't prepared for what I saw in his caramel-colored orbs.

Maybe brown eyes appear more sincere in the way a puppy can get you to share treats without conscious decision. I'm not sure, but I thought I saw a warm regard in his gaze. Interest, and not solely in who would pick up the tab. His scanning look told me this guy might really think me sexy. My brain synapses stuttered.

His slow smile suggested he'd surmised my calculation of his hotness factor. To the tenth decimal. And he didn't mind my interest.

Dedication

This story was a long-time coming.
Thanks to Rhonda Penders,
who asked me to submit when I pitched it years ago,
Judy Jarvie for making sure I completed the book,
and to my beta readers—
Lori Waters, Chris Florky, and Myra Starr.
We did it!

Chapter One

I'd thought time travel novels were light entertainment—implausible, but a great way to learn history. Fun, fictional escapes. My beliefs changed when I experienced reality-altering occurrences bouncing around time. I didn't exactly time travel…but…let me explain.

The strange stuff kicked in right after I saw a psychic for the first time. Having a reading was my neighbor, Chastity Duval's, idea. She insisted my boyfriend cheated on me and thought I'd listen if I learned the truth from a non-involved third party. I went to prove her wrong.

Harteville, North Carolina, is my home. The oldest neighborhood dates to 1780, and boasts narrow streets and brick pavement. A warm sun had shown when I'd arrived there for my reading, but a sudden chill prompted my pulling my collar close. Crisp breezes sent leaves skittering around my feet.

Mouth-watering aromas from a hole-in-the-wall restaurant reminded me I hadn't eaten yet today. I'd been too nervous about this appointment with Madame LaMere. I'd taken off early from work, citing a doctor appointment, and hoped the time I'd have to make up later would be worth the effort.

I found her storefront on a side street, tucked between a patisserie and a coin shop. I'd been up and down this same block before but hadn't previously noticed the deep purple door decorated with gold stars.

Shadows passed over the faded gold-painted window. Block letters spelled out "Madame Myra LaMere, Psychic. Life Readings. Love Foretold. Walk-ins Welcome."

Chills overtook my spine when I grabbed the doorknob. Ignoring the omen, I turned and pushed. A tiny bell chimed when I inched inside.

The small room stood empty but for two straight-backed chairs and a scratched end table. This is where she did her readings? In full view of passers-by? And where was her crystal ball? A multi-hued curtain hid what I suspected was an entrance to her inner sanctum. I couldn't catch my breath, and my aching lungs weren't due to the light incense aroma permeating the space.

"Madame LaMere?"

Shuffled steps, furtive movements and squeaking floorboards preceded the doorway curtain's parting. A woman pushed quietly into the room, stopping close by. Her clear, rosy complexion stirred my envy. If the gray streaks in her hair were an indication, she had passed fifty but looked closer to my age of thirty-three. She wore black leggings, an over-sized blouse, and multiple necklaces. A shawl hung from her crooked elbows.

"You must be Gabby Jung, yes?"

She was psychic and didn't know who I was? This introduction didn't give me a warm, fuzzy feeling. "Yes."

"Today we will use your given name, Gabriella. This way."

Now how had she known my given name? I

shrugged. Perhaps Chastity had spoken with her. My friend has a thing about using full names.

She turned and led the way into a comfortably furnished room. A gray tiger-striped cat jumped off the rumpled window seat cushion and, tail held high, deigned to investigate my shoes. I love cats and have a big tuxedo tom named Cyrano. A fact the feline deduced given her sniff and sedate return to the cushion. The animal's eyes looked fully closed but I could feel her regard.

"Before we begin, I'd like you to take several deep breaths," Madame said. "Your agitation is affecting the auric ethers."

I glanced over the shabby chic chintz and cherry-colored walls, but didn't see anything out of order. I shrugged. What did I know from gases? I breathed deep, feeling marginally better.

Madame hummed then cleared her throat. "Karma. Oh, dear. You have some serious lessons coming soon."

"Karma?"

"The lessons you brought with you into this lifetime."

"Yes, I understand the concept." Chastity had been preaching karma at me for months, though it felt more like lifetimes once she got going. I referred to the concept as caramel to tick her off. Yep, I'm a brat.

"Dharma too." The psychic's voice took on an odd echo, her words reverberating in my ears. "You've set up many responsibilities. It's all coming to a head. Within days."

Icy fingers gripped my gut. "Damn. Why didn't you say so?"

"I did." The woman leaned back, her gaze

speculative. "Parallel lives and alternate dimensions will be involved. You must take care when you find yourself between worlds."

"Oh, right." Whatever the hell "between worlds" meant. The next words jerked from my mouth. "But what about the man of my heart? That's why I'm here. Oh, and my job."

Madame's brow smoothed. She pulled her fringed shawl around her throat, her bejeweled hand holding it tight. "All will work out in Divine Time. Don't worry, you and your true love will live happily ever after. You have obstacles to conquer, first, but I see you triumphing." She frowned. "At this moment, the information is true."

"Don't worry? Don't worry?" I didn't care about repeating myself. I gasped for breath. "Chastity thinks Joel is cheating on me. I damn well do worry about the situation." And my sanity if I'd chosen another low-life to share my bed.

"Joel? Are you sure? I see a dark-haired man. His name starts with an A, or perhaps a C."

My jaw tightened. "Blond. Name begins with J."

"Hmm…dearie, you've got bigger concerns. Unless you always insist on having your way?" She paused in thought. "Although, your true love is part of…no he's integral…no, I'm not sure. We'll have to let that go for now."

"What?" The tiger-striped cat jumped off the rumpled window seat cushion and skittered from the room. I strangled my straining temper. Okay, so maybe I should have used my inside voice.

Madame continued, ignoring my shrewish vocalizations. "Karma, dearie, remember? If you don't reconcile it now, you'll have to deal with it later. In this or some other lifetime."

"Oh, crap."

"Indeed. I see many lifetimes requiring deep healing." She hummed under her breath. "One pivotal timeline may do the trick."

She'd spoken so softly, I wasn't sure I'd heard correctly. Before I could ask for clarification, she moved on. "Once you do the work, your growth will allow you to accept your true love."

The psychic shifted her feet. "You are approaching a life-altering crossroads. Insecurities and anger will hamper you. Choose your companions carefully or suffer the consequences."

"Consequences," I parroted. Oh, Holy Mars Stars.

She leaned forward and grasped my wrist. "Use care. You must heal not only your own lives, but those who touch you most closely, as well. We are all connected in the web of life."

I figured she meant Chastity, who'd insisted we'd been related in many lives.

"Act from your heart," she pointed a slim finger toward my chest, "and not from your head." Her finger shifted direction to match her words. "There are great rewards waiting for you, including the true love your heart desires." She tilted her head. "I also see new employment. Results are up to you."

"But what about—"

"Stop worrying. It will get you nowhere. Be prepared for your challenges to start soon, and ask Chastity for help."

"But how—"

Madame sat back. "This ends the transmission."

"Do you mean you won't answer any more questions?"

"I will give you the responses Spirit wishes you to hear."

"Shoot me now."

I left my payment in a Carnival glass bowl and shut the door firmly on my way out. My thoughts whirled like a manic two-year-old in Santa's workshop. My feet stopped moving. I should have asked Madame more about the mysterious dark-haired man. Where and when would I meet him? And which timeline was most important?

My impromptu statue imitation threw the man in my peripheral vision off balance. He veered to the side, muttering words I ignored as he passed.

Insecurities my ass. I punctuated the thought with a fist to my hip. Okay, I had a few fears, but damn it, didn't everyone? Madame LaMere's fee wasn't inconsiderable. I decided to return and ask for clarification. Maybe I'd finally get what I'd paid for.

I stumbled over a loose brick as I swiveled to return to the storefront. I found the tiny restaurant still exuding tantalizing scents by following my nose. The patisserie and coin shop remained separated by a third storefront. But the deep purple door?

Not in sight.

Madame LaMere's gold-painted window?

Nonexistent.

The third business, the one I'd recently spent thirty minutes inside, sitting on pins, needles, and chintz, had disappeared, along with my hard-earned money.

Oh, Holy Imagination Figment.

****

I kicked my apartment door closed. My black cat clock with the moving tail read six o'clock. Uh oh. Joel would arrive expecting dinner and I hadn't shopped. I could now celebrate an official Crapped Out Day. A knock sounded, doubled up and loud.

"Hang on, I'm coming."

Joel gave me a peck on the cheek and brushed past. "Hey, Gab. What's for dinner?" He settled into my favorite chair and propped his feet on my heirloom coffee table.

"I, uh, I didn't have time to make anything." My anger stirred. "And have you forgotten I asked you to keep your feet off my grandma's table?"

Irritation flickered in his deep blue eyes. His square jaw tightened but he removed his feet. "So what's with no dinner?"

Dark colors tinged with muddy red flashes swirled around his head. I shook my head. What the heck? Must be low blood sugar affecting my vision. I squeezed my eyes closed. When I reopened them, the colors around Joel dissipated. A tight tee displayed his muscled arms and flat stomach. Jeans enfolded his legs like a lover's hand. He cocked his head and smiled, looking like his normal cherubic, blond-haired, blue-eyed self.

My gut clenched. I hate confrontations, but more than once, I've picked men who begin as princes but turn into frogs before hopping away to another woman's pond. I hadn't noticed the pattern until Chastity pointed out my abysmal taste in men.

"Let's go to Mancini's. Eggplant Parmesan is today's special."

He ran his fingers through his curly hair then stood. "You don't mind buying tonight do you? I've had a few extra bills this week."

I smothered the angry thoughts about him watching his money and spending mine for the last several months. Now where had the irritation come from? I'd never minded helping out before. Wasn't Joel's fault he'd been down-sized.

Joel smoothed his fingers over my forehead, his pupils darkening as he bent to kiss me. He moved his lips to my cheekbones and across to my ear. "I'll buy next time."

I bit back my ire and maneuvered him out the door. "Come on. If we go now we'll beat the crowd."

When had my life gone to shit without my notice? I locked the door and followed Joel downstairs and out. He wrapped his muscled arm around me and pulled me close, his familiar heat dissipating my funk.

I snuggled close, our hips bouncing off each other. So we weren't always in step. All couples have problems. Everything would be fine once he found a job.

Soon. Hadn't Madame LaMere said I had great rewards coming?

Okay then. Unless I'd dreamed my interaction with the older woman.

We jolted down the block and into Mancini's.

Chapter Two

Garlic. Onions. Olive Oil. Three scents guaranteeing my mouth would water. My stomach growling as I walked through the door was simply affirmation I'd arrived in gustatory heaven.

Mancini's occupied a long, narrow space in an old brick building. Antique couches arranged along each of the two long walls were fronted with mismatched tables and chairs. The noise volume should have been high given the number of people jammed in together, but somehow the acoustics worked. Harteville's best Italian food, along with the owner's bonhomie, made the intimate seating seem like a big family dinner.

I shrugged off my jacket, glad we'd made it before the nightly waiting line formed.

Mario, the restaurant's owner, enfolded me in a hug. "*Il mio amico*, you've come for my eggplant, eh? You're in luck, I have one table left."

Ignoring Joel and not waiting for my answer, Mario grabbed two menus and wove between tightly packed tables. "Your server will be right with you." He left the menus. A bus boy ran over with two filled water glasses.

Throwing my jacket across my chair's back, I glanced over the room. We'd gotten the last table, but I recognized luck had a price. The other customers were reading menus and watching for a waiter, as we were. I hoped my boyfriend wouldn't notice and we'd luck out with a quick server.

"I thought you said we'd beat the crowd," Joel said. "This place is mobbed. It'll take forever."

"We're seated. We have menus." I looked toward the door. "And see, the line is already out the door. We're ahead of all those people." He didn't lift his head to look, so I put my hand over his to gain his attention. He slid it away and grabbed his water.

Uh oh. My stomach muscles clenched. The night was not going as I'd hoped. "Would you share the eggplant special with me?" My voice sounded more strained than I'd like.

"Geez, Gab. I thought you were cooking and I saved my appetite. Splitting an entrée won't do it. Besides, I need something with meat."

My jaw tightened. "I don't get paid until Friday, and I had a large cash outlay today."

"If you'd have cooked, you wouldn't have to watch your pennies. Restaurants are always more expensive than making something at home."

I didn't answer. I'd planned on a PB&J for dinner, forgetting he'd be eating with me. Again. As if he didn't stop by three nights in five. Maybe I should invest in a flashing neon sign proclaiming, "Eat at Gabby's." My jaw tightened. These new thoughts about Joel's parsimony made my stomach rock and roll.

Joel glanced at me. "Sure, hon, splitting a special sounds fine." He reached across the table and took my hand in his. "I can spring for an appetizer." He smiled at me. "Okay?"

"Surc. Sorry I'm so crabby. I'm not super hungry, so the appetizer is all yours."

"Great." He transferred his smile, and his hand, to the menu.

Had Joel put my back up tonight, or did the memory of those red flashes I'd seen unsettle me? I needed an attitude adjustment, the kind I could best get with a glass of Chianti.

A blonde waitress stopped at the table next to ours. "Finally," Joel said. We've been waiting for someone to show. A guy could die of thirst before you get around to doing your job."

She smiled and answered without missing a beat. "Sir, your server will be right with you." She pointed at the table before her with her pen. "This is a different section."

I glanced at our neighbors, with what I knew was a red face and an apologetic smile plastered on my lips.

Holy Cannoli. Nope, a quick eye blink didn't change the sight. One of the two men next to us had a body by Adonis, a face by Hollywood, and damn, they worked well together. Dark brown hair pulled back in a short ponytail, high cheekbones, full lips, and laughing eyes the color of a mocha latte drew my full attention. My "Stud-A-Month" calendar needed him on the cover. I wouldn't mind him gracing every month, either.

Sure, I dated Joel monogamously, but no warm-blooded woman could come upon this scenic view without stopping for a Kodak moment. He even seemed familiar in a seen-around-the-neighborhood way. I wondered if his name began with an "A" or a "C." Nope, the psychic had a screw lose. If I hadn't dreamed her.

"Well that sucks," Joel said. "Switch us to your section then."

11

I turned my gaze back in time to see Joel employ his mega-wattage smile, and not with me. "Hunger does strange things to people. A beautiful server like you could satisfy my needs." As if he remembered I sat watching, he dialed back. "For food, I mean. We're really hungry."

Mario appeared with a concerned look on his face. "Is there a problem?"

Joel waved his hands in the air. "Yeah, we're hungry. What's taking so long?"

"We arrived less than five minutes ago. Everyone came at about the same time," I said. "I don't mind waiting my turn, Mario."

Mario's lips straightened. "I will wait on you."

Orders were placed and wine served. I thought a scene had been averted. Until the neighboring table's resident god leaned toward us. He caught Joel's attention with a tap on his arm.

"You know, if I had a beautiful, sexy woman like yours, I'd treat her the way she deserved rather than embarrassing her by coming on to the server in front of her. Or even behind her back."

His brown gaze entangled mine. "No offense, sweets, but you look too intelligent to stick yourself with low-rent goods."

I don't know if I'd have responded even if the royal blue light emanating from around his hands and head hadn't caught my eye. My elbow rested on the table with my chin in my hand for a better look in a fluid motion I hadn't known I could execute.

In what seemed a totally natural move, my gaze traveled from the light phenomenon to Mr. Calendar's eyes. If I thought I'd been hypnotized by the blue marvel, I wasn't prepared for what I saw in his caramel-colored orbs.

Maybe brown eyes appear more sincere in the way a puppy can get you to share treats without conscious decision. I'm not sure, but I thought I saw a warm regard in his gaze. Interest, and not solely in who would pick up the tab. His scanning look told me this guy might really think me sexy. My brain synapses stuttered.

His slow smile suggested he'd surmised my calculation of his hotness factor. To the tenth decimal. And he didn't mind my interest. I stared until Joel's irritated growl gained my attention.

I turned from the sapphire haze and ducked the glower I anticipated on Joel's face by gulping half a glass of wine at one go. Perhaps not a smart move on an empty stomach, but necessary. By the time I lowered my drink, it appeared the two men had opted to ignore each other. Hunger, prodded by a newly delivered basket of bread and a plate of dipping oil, must have won out over machismo.

Keeping my attention on my food, I avoided catching the eye of either Joel or Mr. Calendar. Nope, didn't want to see colors around either man.

After a short wait, our hot food was delivered and split between us. Although my dinner looked and smelled fabulous, and my stomach clamored for food, I continued thinking about my reading with Madame L. Had she been right about Joel? And what about the scene between Joel and the waitress? I pushed worry from my mind and wondered what hallucinations meant when I'd never used psychedelic substances.

Joel snapped his fingers in my face. "Earth to

Gab."

"What."

"You gonna finish yours?" He pointed his fork at my largely uneaten eggplant special.

I exchanged my plate with his empty one. "Go ahead."

"So, what's biting your…bothering you?"

"I told you, I had a tough day," I said, conscious of Mr. Calendar's not-so-hidden regard. Mario must have used too much salt in the eggplant, or else the furnace was set too high. I finished off my water wishing I could afford more wine.

"So I'll buy you a second damn glass," Joel said.

"Huh? Oh, thanks."

Now the hallucinations were both visual and auricular. Great.

"Gab, you know I'm on unemployment. I have to watch my money until I find a job."

I glanced from the corner of my eye. Mr. Calendar kept his head down, but, yes, I saw enough of his grin to know he eavesdropped.

"I get your situation Joel, but—" I swallowed hard. My courage spurt flagged. My hand reached tentatively for his arm. I stopped, hovering before retracting my gesture. "Never mind."

Joel gulped his drink, twirled the empty wine glass by its stem then set it down. Red wine tendrils ran down the inside of the glass.

"Sorry, Gab." He leaned forward sporting a smile reminding me of an oil slick on wet pavement. "You know I'm tense because of the job situation, right?" He patted my hand. "I don't mean to take it out on you." He leaned toward me. "Tell you what, I've got a few dollars set aside for job search gas money. I'll use it to pay half the meal along with your second glass of wine."

Joel seemed to know when he'd pushed me too far, even when I didn't verbally protest. This was one of those times.

Up to now, I'd accepted my boyfriend's apologies. Tonight's interactions prodded my thoughts. Perhaps I settled for too little. Chastity had told me the same thing for weeks, but I hadn't listened, sure she was wrong. Combined with Madame L's earlier pronouncements, the eerie colors I saw, and Joel's asinine behavior tonight, I wondered if the worm had turned. The night crawler in question being me.

The noise level increased. Several people waiting in line looked like they wanted to push us from our chairs. I knew the feeling and figured the servers would like a chance to earn more tips.

"Joel, let's go. Mario could use the table."

"Fine." He finished off my wine and stood, his eyes on our neighbors. "He could also use better customers."

Mr. Calendar's lips curved up, but he kept his attention on the tiramisu before him. His companion, a second calendar worthy man, had coffee and a liqueur. My mouth watered at the sight, and not from the gustatory treats I spied.

Good thing Mr. C. didn't reply to Joel's comment. I'd be hard pressed to side with my lover.

Outside Mancini's I breathed in the cool autumnal air.

"So, Gab, I have an interview tomorrow. You don't mind if we make it an early night, do you?"

Normally when he didn't stay the night, I'd worry I'd done something wrong. Tonight, only a sardonic quip came to mind. I squashed my reply.

A break from Joel would be timely. I needed space to determine why I stayed with a man who no longer made me his sole focus. He had treated me so well at first. We'd shared dinners—he paid—and a hot sex life. Then, so slowly I hadn't noticed, he'd stopped treating and started expecting. The sex had fallen like an avalanche, too.

Though leaving Joel after he'd seen me through a difficult patch hadn't crossed my mind until today. Loyalty counted in my world.

"Gab? Something wrong?" He jiggled the keys in his pocket. "I've gotta go."

"I've had a long day, remember?" I hugged his stiff body, not unaware he hated affectionate displays in public. Instead of backing off as usual, I went up on tiptoes and planted a kiss on his lips. Take that, you bugger. "See you around, Joel."

"Wait, what did you say?"

I ignored him calling my name and hurried into the near dark. The stranger I'd labeled Mr. Calendar stood front and center in my mind, his image pictured in detail. His comments cycled through my thoughts. "Beautiful, sexy woman…treat her the way she deserved."

Damn, but I couldn't help wondering what he considered appropriate treatment.

Chapter Three

"Gabriella!" Chastity Duval swept in to my living room the next morning. Her embroidered silk kimono streamed behind her six-foot runway model-sized frame.

"So, Gabriella, tell me about your reading. Isn't she like the best psychic you've ever met? I just *love* Madame LaMere. She is so *sweet*."

I sent my neighbor a scowl then scolded myself and smiled. Chastity couldn't help her Pollyanna attitude—her parents were hippies, past and present. But I wished she wouldn't speak in italics. Sometimes it made my teeth hurt.

"Well, Chast, the reading didn't go quite as I expected." I ignored her pout, hoping I wouldn't hear the "vibration of names" lecture. Again. Chastity's belief names held special energy didn't click with me. Neither did astrology, numerology, tarot, or the rest of Chastity's alternative stuff. How we'd become friends was a life mystery I'd accepted without question.

"I'm at a karmic crossroads." I winced. I hadn't intended to broach the scary topic.

Chastity's mouth dropped into the traditional fly catching position. After a moment, it wobbled into an O shape. "Wow. Oh, Gabriella, that's *amazing*. What did she tell you? No, wait, let me make some detox tea first. You need to clear your negativity. I'll be right back."

She left the apartment before I could stop her, the dragon on her kimono fluttering.

Well, I figured I lucked out, and she wouldn't be pushing the thick green drink smelling like old fish on me. Plus, tea is easier to toss. I looked over my shoulder at the palm tree I used to dump my friend's weird concoctions. It looked surprisingly healthy so the drinks couldn't be all bad…for trees.

"Now where were we?" Chastity returned, her appearance overwhelming my apartment's small living room. She pushed a brightly glazed ceramic mug at me. "Let's get settled, I want to hear *every word*."

My nostrils picked up the tea's scent. My stomach rebelled. The special cleanse blend made the fishy green drink smell like high-end perfume. Only something appeared different today. A golden glow surrounded the mug. Strange. I pretended to sip.

Chastity meant well. Genuine and genuinely gorgeous. My five-foot-five inches and mousy red-brown hair didn't match up. We weren't exactly Mutt and Jeff when we traveled together—men didn't see anyone but Chastity. And I didn't envy my friend…often. Seemed my self-esteem hadn't had far to drop before hitting the gutter today, and my rising guilt about mentally sniping at Chastity didn't help my peace of mind.

My neighbor's voice interrupted my thoughts.

"Gabriella? Remember. Tell me *every word*."

"You know I went to ask about Joel but Madame LaMere ignored my question. Instead, she talked about 'karma and dharma, alternative lives and parallel dimensions.'" My fingers air quoted the psychic's words. "I really don't give a flying—"

Chastity tutted and shook her finger at me.

"Nuh, uh, uh. We've talked about this. Words have vibrations. You need to use *good* words to create *positive* vibrations."

Shit. The vibrations lecture. Damn it all to hell.

I hummed under my breath and went to the happy place in my mind my neighbor had insisted I create for stressful times. I love my friend, but there are occasions I want to whimper in private. Like now.

"Gabriella? Gabriella! Listen. This is *important*. What exactly did Madame LaMere tell you?"

I sighed. My happy place of cool mountain streams and meadows filled with blooming wild flowers under sunny, clear blue skies faded. I collapsed against the couch back with a moan and repeated what I could remember.

"You need to prepare. I'll help you."

Crapola. It didn't take a psychic to know more thick green stuff loomed on the horizon. I'd drink it—a small portion—to make my friend happy. The stuff didn't do a damn thing.

Chastity plunked her mug onto a coaster. "I'm surprised Madame didn't tell you to dump Joel. He's not right for you."

"Truly the only good news I had. She told me I'd live happily ever after with my true love."

My neighbor's expression perked up, a small smile curved her lips. "She said true love?"

I pushed down my irritation. Chastity had never hidden her dislike of Joel but I had enough on my plate without replaying our old argument.

"Yes, true love. Why?"

Chastity leaned forward and placed her mug on the

table. "Her words mean it's not Joel. Oh, *goody*."

"Hey, come on. That's my boyfriend you're trashing." Maybe Chastity was right about his womanizing, but until I knew for sure, Joel deserved my loyalty.

I sighed. I really hated my inability to confront life's nasty side. If Madame L were right, I'd be forced to change sooner than later. I wasn't sure how I felt. Maybe I'd get lucky and my life would improve without too much disruption.

"Give me a clue, oh Professor of Mysteries. What do I do now? I have the feeling there aren't any support groups or twelve step programs to contact."

She sank into the cushions, pulling her long legs up under her. "Actually?"

I leaned forward ready to give my entire attention to Chastity's sage words.

She cleared her throat. "Well, no there aren't."

"Ah, shi—oot."

"Why, what's wrong? You look greener than Kermit." She rubbed her nose. "Sorry. I'm just sayin'."

"Do you know, I mean, is it normal to um, see stuff?"

My friend leaned forward. "What haven't you told me?"

I squirmed. This was harder than I thought it'd be. "Colors. I'm seeing colors and sometimes multiple colors. Around, you know, around people. Sometimes animals."

I'd seen emerald green around Cyrano earlier today. He must be deep in sleep not to have sensed Chastity's entry. He normally claimed her lap the moment she sat.

I inhaled. "Is seeing extra colors normal? 'Cause it's making me crazy."

"Auras!" My friend crowed, "Oh, you lucky girl!"

At least I had a name for the phenomena. Auras. I'd heard the term and ignored the concept.

"So what can you tell me about auras?" I winced at the last word. This was well out of my comfort zone.

Chastity wiggled and rubbed her hands together. "Oh, boy, I never thought I'd hear you ask me about auras. This is great."

I sighed. "Get on with this, please. Put me out of my misery."

"It's simple, really. Auras are fields surrounding all living things on Earth. Some people say in the Universe, but I don't want to push you."

I rolled my eyes at the ceiling.

"Anyway, aura colors are related to emotions, physical conditions and thoughts of the being you're observing. Auras change all the time and can be a combination of colors. The clearer, lighter colors are positive vibes. Stay away from dark or muddy auras." She paused. "So tell me, what did you see?"

I remembered the tea's glow. "Golden, golden sparkles."

"Wow, divine guidance. It could also mean wisdom or protection. Depends on what else appears."

I eyed Chastity's tea. Drinking the unidentifiable stuff led to enlightenment? Oh, come on. I swallowed the cooling liquid. Wait a minute. If auras only showed around living beings, what the heck was in this tea? I shoved the cup back onto the table.

"What else have you seen?"

I recalled the glow coming from the man sitting

beside me last night. "Blue. A clear sapphire and cobalt blue combination."

"Honey, that's a being you can trust and love. Was it a dog? Dogs often have blue around them."

"A guy." I laughed. "Before you ask, I have no idea who he was. I tried concentrating on seeing only what I know is real."

My friend huffed. "Auras are real."

"To you, yes. To me they're scary shit." I interpreted her raised eyebrows and amended "shit" to "stuff." "So tell me, what does all this mean?"

A loud double knock sounded at the door.

"Chastity? I think maybe we'd better pick up 'Metaphysics 101' later."

My neighbor's mouth twisted into an unattractive moue. "It's him, isn't it? When are you going to—"

Another knock, this time louder.

"Never mind. I'll go gladly knowing a certain man is on his way out."

Chastity unfolded her body and glided to the door, throwing it open as Joel's fist was poised to make contact with the wood panel. He staggered forward.

I stifled my quick grin. Chastity had impeccable timing and Joel had fallen into her trap more than once.

Joel regained his balance as she swept out. He slammed the door. Pulling down his tee's hem, he gave me a peck on the cheek.

"Aren't those the clothes you wore last night? And didn't you want an early night to prep for an interview today?"

He shrugged. "No clean laundry. Besides, I was in a hurry to see you. I'll change later."

His smile beamed. I relaxed. He hadn't asked to

use my washer-dryer. Maybe he'd come by just to say hello for a change. Perhaps he'd morphed back into the charming man I'd known.

"Hey, Gab. You've got the morning off today, right? What's for breakfast?"

Cyrano stalked into the room, spotted Joel, puffed his fur, and hissed. Oh, happy day.

Chapter Four

Later that night I jerked awake, my thoughts spinning faster than the room did when I drank too much tequila. Rolling onto my side, I rubbed my eyes. The clock's LED display read four ten. Groaning, I flopped onto my back. I bent my left knee and rested my right arm across my forehead in my preferred thinking posture.

Being alone didn't totally suck, but the unknown? So what if Madame LaMere had insisted my future differed from what I'd expected. What did the psychic know? She could go whistle Dixie or whatever other song—

A soft click sounded in the dark and a strange light flickered.

I froze.

Then I heard a low hum. Maybe the refrigerator's motor acted up again. My feet swept the bed from side-to-side, feeling for Cyrano. His sprawling form didn't cover my bed's lower half, as usual. He chose to sleep elsewhere when Joel stayed, but Joel had bailed. After I'd made him breakfast, he'd gone home to change for his interview and I hadn't seen him since. I briefly wondered how his meeting had gone.

The flickering light appeared centered in my living room. I eased from my bed, donned a warm robe, and followed the beckoning, sparkling glow. I blinked.

What the hell?

The living room was the same size and shape. Windows were in the same places. But nothing else looked familiar other than Cyrano draped over the couch's back. Or what should have been the shabby couch I know and hate. The sofa now placed in my apartment resembled the one I'd salivated over in a design magazine last month.

Bluish-white light gleamed with a soft silver radiance emanating from the center. A woman sat on my "not couch," clicking her long acrylic fingernails rhythmically on the glass tabletop.

"Ahhh." I swallowed past a dry lump. "Excuse me?" My voice sounded weak, ineffectual to my ears. I cleared my throat. "Hello?"

Couch Woman ignored my verbal overtures. Instead, as if she couldn't hear me, she leaned into the cushions in a familiar pose, her left leg bent at the knee.

I studied her, hit with a faint sense of recognition. The honey colored highlights and shiny red-brown hair were the results of an expensive hairdresser rather than nature. Clothes cut to make the most of the stranger's curvy yet fit figure did their job. She looked casually sexy. A style I'd love to call my own if I felt comfortable spending instead of saving money.

I scanned the room searching for familiar items. New furniture had replaced my early attic décor. Stylish club chairs and the afore-mentioned sofa invited people to sit and relax. A free-standing gas fireplace stood against the wall; merry but soundless flames lit the room. Again, something I wished I owned, especially given this autumn's cool, damp weather.

The mantel held art glass and a framed photograph.

A handsome man, lanky, with dark brown hair and high cheekbones stared from the picture. His tan skin and brown eyes drew my eye. He looked familiar. Damn, it was Mr. Calendar.

I shook my head and pinched myself. It hurt. Couldn't be a dream. Unless a person could convince herself the pinch hurt when it didn't. I'd ask Chastity.

Approaching the woman, my head swam and my stomach jumped. I put my hands on my hips and raised my voice. "Who are you?" I leaned forward. "Why are you in my house?"

No answer. Ignored as if I didn't exist. What was up with the woman?

Cyrano jumped from the couch and wound himself around my legs. Okay, so my cat was real. Maybe. He slipped past me.

"Cyrano?" He looked over his shoulder and walked to the bedroom. So if he could see and hear me, why didn't the woman respond?

Before I could shake my unwelcome guest's tree again, the space shimmered like heat waves rising from hot asphalt. As I watched, the scene I thought I saw faded, supplanted by my living room's normal view.

I rubbed my eyes. What the? I must have been sleepwalking. No vestige of my waking dream remained. Too bad. The fireplace resembled a photo I'd ripped from a dentist's office magazine. Don't get on my case. We've all done something similar.

Maybe I'd lost a few more brain cells when I'd finished off a half bottle of wine earlier tonight. Last night. Again—whatever.

Right. Keep repeating yourself, sister. Listening to Chastity's lectures on creating reality from thoughts didn't mean accepting her ideology. I returned to my bedroom. As I reached the door, I looked over my shoulder. A flicker caught my peripheral vision. I grabbed the baseball bat I keep handy and turned toward my living room. As I advanced, the flicker disappeared with an audible click.

Oh, shit. I ran back to my bedroom and jumped beneath the covers clutching my bat. Cyrano pounced beside me, his head butting the top of my head.

The recent sights didn't scare me, much, but what the hell was happening? I placed my palm over my pounding heart and forced air into my lungs. Cyrano's purr worked his calming magic and my pulse and thoughts slowed to make sense of what I'd seen.

I splayed my fingers through his black and white fur, the irony of his coloring clear. The world I'd always viewed as having clear lines was disappearing. Good thing I still had my trusty cat to help make sense of the world. Cyrano and Chastity. Too bad it was too late, or rather, too early to wake my neighbor. Chastity didn't function before ten a.m. and often didn't turn on her phone until noon.

Even though I couldn't see strange things from under covers pulled to my hairline, I figured I wouldn't see danger coming, either. I sat against the headboard, wrestling the bat from under the covers.

Holy Hallucinations. My brain ran in circles, trying to process what I'd seen. I kept checking the time, which alternated between a creeping pace and a rush toward dawn.

My brain had begun winding down when a loud click caught my attention. Cyndi Lauper singing "Time After Time" blared from my clock radio.

Heart pounding, I pushed past the half-folded quilt and stumbled from bed, my robe wrapped around my knees. Grabbing my baseball bat, I walked the few paces to my living room. Should be safe to look in daylight, right?

A slash of red sky visible through my window illuminated the room that hadn't changed since I'd moved in several years earlier. The furniture remained a rummage sale collection. It didn't hold a gas fireplace. The walls I kept planning to paint remained dingy white.

I staggered and caught myself with a hand on the doorframe. My memories could be attributed to dreams if it weren't for the bat and my groggy thought processes. I shook my head. Damn. It better not be dharma-karma chameleon stuff brought on by Madame LaMere's warning. I rubbed my upper arms. The whole scene last night had to be a weird illusion.

Checking the living room once again and shaking my head, I shuffled into the tiny kitchen, hitting the on switch of my prepped coffee maker. Then I sleepwalked through my morning routine.

"Strange night caused by too much vino. I won't get all hung up with woo-woo crap." Even if the hazy colors surrounding my hands looked way too much like the blue-white flickers from my dream.

A freaking realistic dream, but hey, they happen sometimes.

I bade Cyrano good-bye and stumbled down the building's stairs yawning. "Dang, I can't wake up this morning." I halted on the landing. "Maybe I'm not really awake." I pinched myself. "Ouch, okay, question answered."

Coffee. I needed more coffee, damn the budget.

I pushed through the door and headed across the street. Head down, I turned at The Ground Up Coffeehouse entrance.

"Hey, hold on, sweetheart. I don't feel like wearing my coffee."

I stopped inches from a pair of large white running shoes. My gaze moved from the shoes, past nicely fitted jeans, over a loose tee that managed to hug muscled arms and up to the face I remembered too well.

Mr. C. held a coffee cup in each hand. "I figured you didn't want to try on my hot drinks for size, either."

My body absorbed his low voice like warm honey poured over baklava hot from the oven but his words escaped me. What had he said? I squinted. Could he be—?

He moved to one side and gestured with a grande-sized container. "Would you mind moving? I'd open the door for you but—"

Mind? Hell no. I peeped through my sunglasses. *Wait a minute.* Oh, now I got it. The dream continued using my fixation on the man from Mancini's as inspiration.

His lips curved up at the corners, his head tilted to one side. "The way the sunlight hits your hair reminds me of Titian's *Venus of Urbino.*"

Oh, now I *knew* I dreamed. *Right.* Like a demi-god would want anything to do with me, much less compare me to a classical painting. Yes, my red-brown hair could be called Titian, but I'd long considered it a poor version of auburn. My hazel eyes are okay, and my features are in line with my face size, so I'd considered myself regular. But painting model worthy? I scrutinized his face, looking for signs of low intelligence or a con man's shifty expression. His warm expression left me a bit nonplused.

"You're joking, right? I'd ask you to pinch me, but your hands are full. So, am I dreaming? I guess I could pinch myself to see, right?"

He checked the container tops and sipped from one. A grande cappuccino. My kind of coffee guy.

"Not sure why you think you're dreaming, and I'd kiss you awake before I'd pinch you."

"Now I know I'm dreaming. First I saw you at the restaurant, then in my dream last night."

"You dreamed about me?" He grinned. "Then we'll see each other again."

"In your dreams." Huh? Could I have said anything dumber?

"I really do need to leave or I'll be late." He motioned with the cups. ""Do you mind letting me by?"

His comment about being late jogged my brain. "Oh, sorry. Yes. I'm a bit slow this morning. I didn't get much sleep last night."

"Good to know I kept you awake the same way you kept me tossing and turning. See you later, dream girl."

Backing from the doorway, I watched my male fantasy move out of sight.

I shook my head and scrounged in my purse for change. Even though my heart already beat double time, I needed an extra shot of espresso. I had a project report due to my boss by noon, and would be pushing to meet my deadline. Me operating on less than a full night's sleep meant my day could become nightmarish.

My boss Howie Jackson had made it clear last

Friday that he watched my work closely. He deserves the title of dipshit more than the department supervisor one he holds. The things he doesn't know about accounts receivable office procedure would be scary if his lack of brains wasn't so typical of life in a large corporation. Chastity says my intelligence scares Howie. I don't know. I think he's a classic corporate dickwad, promoted because he's a champion ass-kisser. Oh, and maybe because he's a shirt-tail relation to the Jacksons in Jackson and Jackson Accounting, a large regional firm and my employer.

All I know is if a person's true worth were shown in their face and body, Howie Jackson would look like a shriveled cow pie. Instead, he's brown-haired and blue-eyed with a ready smile. His six plus feet of handsome is housed in a quarterback's body. He uses his looks to charm his superiors and his fit body to loom over people who are smaller in stature. He didn't impress me and he knew it.

My work buddy, Donna Morris, keeps the office going, the unsung hero of J&J Accounting. She's cleaned up Howie's messes so often we've taken to calling her The Sweeper. I knew she was on my side, but she wouldn't be able to save my ass if I didn't come up with the billing information and graphs Howie needed by noon to wow his upper-level manager.

The ordering line at The Ground Up was so long I almost reconsidered leaving and making do with the colored water Howie passed off as coffee. Because he always arrived before anyone else and seemed to have an early warning system when more coffee needed brewing, no one else got a crack at the machine. A jaw-cracking yawn settled the question, and I slid into my cubicle ten minutes past my official start time.

Donna leaned her short, sturdy body against a wall panel and crossed her arms. Today she wore her long black hair in a neat braid. A bluish red wool jacket played up her peaches and cream complexion and gray eyes. She was not only The Sweeper but the reason I stayed at J&J. Corporate politics was bearable with her at my side.

"I hate to bring bad tidings so early in the day, but Howie was looking for you ten minutes ago," she said. "I told him you were in the bathroom."

I rubbed my eyes. "What does the Grand Poobah want? Besides further ruining the start of an already shitty day? Good thing it's Friday."

"Shh." Donna looked both ways. "Don't let him hear. I couldn't bear to lose you, too."

Donna's words hit my shame meter, ratcheting the scale to high. "Sorry," I muttered. "What's wrong? You know I wouldn't be late without a good reason."

"I hope your report is done," she said.

"Not quite." I yawned. "Sorry, didn't get much sleep. Why? What's up?"

"Howie said the report deadline was moved up to ten." Donna's forehead pulled into a frown. "You'll be ready, right?"

Anger flooded me. "What an asswipe." I fought to moderate my tone when Donna made shushing motions. "Shit. He didn't give me the final numbers until five o'clock last night. He knows I can't possibly be done."

"Let me help," she said.

I knew she had her own work, but given Howie's underhanded dealings with those he didn't like, she understood he'd played dirty. I was sure he'd lied about the noon deadline from the get go so I'd planned ahead, but couldn't meet the new time without assistance.

"Will you help me double check the data? I've got the graphs complete but for the final numbers, so finishing up won't take long." Given Donna's raised eyebrows, she'd inferred what I hadn't said. Howie had tripped up more than one person with his evil ways and data tampering.

The adrenaline rush did what drinking two coffees hadn't, and we completed the reports with ten minutes to spare. Not trusting myself, or my boss, I e-mailed the report to Howie, with a blind copy to Donna at two minutes to ten. I'd met the deadline and he had no time to change my report.

To calm down and improve my attitude, I accompanied Donna on her smoke break. I've never gotten the hang of smoking, but I wanted to talk privately with her. Inhaling second hand smoke after the favor she'd done was a teeny price.

We hustled to the doorway designated for smokers, and I was relieved we had the entrance to ourselves.

"Thanks for covering and for checking the report numbers, Donna."

Her cheeks hollowed as she sucked on her cancer stick. "No problem." She exhaled a smoke cloud. "Good thing you thought to check the data. I couldn't believe the errors we found."

"I could." I wrapped my arms across my chest to ward off the chilly breeze. "He's pulled the same crap before."

Her fingers stilled with her cigarette poised at her lips. She shook her head quickly before taking another pull. Her attention focused on a point across the street.

"I don't know what I'd do without you here."

I leaned against the brick wall behind me. "I don't know what I'd do without you, period. That's why I think you should start your own business and take me with you."

Donna sighed and studied her cigarette. Her shoulders bowed and she folded her arms.

Dark yellow with tinges of brown appeared around her shoulders, and splashes of lemon yellow showed around her head. What the hell could those colors mean? I had a feeling Donna was feeling Howie's pressure yet wasn't ready to take a chance on leaving J&J. Heck, I'd suspected as much from her body language, even without seeing her aura. I went with my gut.

"You always pooh-pooh me, but you know the smaller accounts would follow if you left. Some mid-size firms too. Why don't you take a chance? You could provide a perfect niche for the customers J&J neglects. Being your own boss would be scary, sure, but you'd have control over your life for a change."

"Tom Jackson would shut me down in a heartbeat," she said. "It's conflict of interest for an accounts liaison to walk taking a client list with her. Them treating their smaller customers poorly wouldn't matter. Luring J&J accounts would constitute a lawsuit type problem."

"What if you went to work for a new firm and clients left on their own? What then?"

"Even if another firm existed in Harteville, I'd likely not earn what I'm making now, so why would I move?"

The lemon yellow around her head sparked then the colors disappeared. A shadow blocked the sun. I rubbed my arms with the sudden chill. "I hear you. Still, I think you're too smart to go on making J&J rich while they pay you a pittance. You deserve better. Besides, then you could hire me."

She crushed her cigarette beneath her heel. "Same to you. When you form your dream company, employ me to keep your books."

My fantasy company would finance creative folks and *their* dreams. "It's a deal."

I have an accounting degree going begging because I don't want to move to a large city. I grew up in Hartville. My extended family was here, though my parents had moved to Arizona after inheriting my aunt's ostrich farm. People I'd known all my life kept me here. Job choices were limited in Harteville, and Howie used the knowledge. If I could get my business going, I'd help more than creative folks.

After going off break, I called Chastity but didn't reach her. Then Howie returned from his meeting, piling on so much work I didn't have time to think much less call my friend. So when I saw her waiting outside my apartment, a load of stress dropped from my shoulders.

Chapter Five

A stack of thick books rested at Chastity's feet. My shoulders tensed again. If any of the book's titles ended with "ology," I'd bolt, but not before unloading my worries regarding Disappearing Couch Woman, Mr. Calendar, and aura color meanings.

"Gabriella, I'm *so* glad you're home."

"Me, too. It's been a tough day. What's with the books?" I felt my curiosity stir despite myself. Some of the volumes looked ancient, with cracked covers and sprung bindings. Sticky notes erupted in a colorful fan from three sides of most tomes.

"Research. I promised I'd help you, and here it is. The fruit of my day."

"I'd rather have a mango."

"Silly. It's a good thing I know you're only *teasing*." She tossed her head full of perfect blonde hair. "I know you're uncomfortable with the situation you face, so I got busy."

"You did all this?" A rush of shame filled my chest, heating my face.

My friend's eyebrows met over her nose. "Well, sure. I know you'd help me if I were in trouble. It's the least I can do."

I dropped my handbag, enfolding my neighbor in a tight hug. I don't agree with most of Chastity's ideas, but how could I not appreciate her enthusiasm?

"Thanks. I mean it, Chast…ity. You're the best."

"Um, you may not like the path you face." She gently broke the hug. "But I've got some great stuff for you."

I shook my head, resigned to a conversation filled with odd words and stranger ideas. Perhaps the unrelieved boredom I'd feel with the discussion meant I'd sleep through the night.

Unlocking the door, I tipped my head to the side in invitation. "Come on in. And let me carry half those books. I don't want you getting a hernia."

Her arm muscles didn't even flex as she bent and picked up the stack. "No problem. I've been working out."

"I see."

"You relax, I'll make you some tea."

I threw a guilty look toward the palm tree. "Sit and relax. I'll get us something from the fridge. Beer okay or would you rather have a glass of red wine?"

"Water is good. I must concentrate. There are several conflicting versions and other important details I shouldn't forget."

I gulped, wishing I could unleash the big guns like chocolate martinis or margaritas. I settled for a glass of wine and a seat on the couch.

"Can you give me the Karma for Dummies version?"

Chastity turned the bindings toward her and ran her finger down the stack. "I don't remember seeing an orange book for any of these subjects."

I sighed. My cranky self had come out to kvetch again. "Sorry. I'm being a bitch."

She jumped to her feet. "You're *hungry*. I've got

appetizers ready next door. I'll be right back."

My head dropped against the sofa cushion, and I closed my eyes. I didn't want to deal with these topics ever, much less now.

Chastity swept into the room with a platter of cheese, crackers, and fruit.

I blinked and surreptitiously sniffed, remembering the time she'd attempted palming off rice and tofu as cheese. This didn't smell funky and even looked like real cheese.

"Yes, it's the real thing. I broke down and bought dairy for you. Don't blame *me* when your sinuses are blocked with mucus."

I rubbed my hands together in anticipation. "Ohboyohboy. Thanks." The plate emptied quickly and I rubbed my stomach. "I owe you."

My friend's assessing gaze moved over my face. "Your color is better, so if you're ready, I'll tell you what I know so far."

My stomach muscles clenched. "Okay, let's get on with it."

Chastity opened a thin-lined notebook. She held up her index finger. "First, I'm going to jump right into the deep water, so let me know when you're drowning."

I blew out my cheeks as if holding my breath and put my hand up over my head.

My friend ignored my theatrics and checked her notes. "Okay, maybe the easiest way to start is by explaining reincarnation using quantum mechanics."

I felt my eyes roll. I hadn't intended on making that expression, but couldn't control myself. Chastity grabbed my shoulder and tightened her grip. "I get that you aren't interested in my beliefs. I'm trying to help.

You."

Chastened, I sat up straight. "Sorry. Go ahead."

"Fine. Many worlds co-exist simultaneously with ours."

My forehead creased. "I know. Life in outer space. Got it."

"No, I mean other dimensions."

"Got that too. Time is one dimension; I forget the others. Maybe space?"

"Listen. Some people, including Einstein, believe all time occurs simultaneously."

My brain seized. "Huh? Are you saying there's no such thing as past or future?"

Chastity clapped her hands. "Yes! You're such a fast *learner*!"

"But that's, that's...hard to grasp." My attention fragmented with the reasoning. "I mean, how do you know where you are?"

"It's easy. The only 'real world' is the one you concentrate on at the moment."

Could last night's disappearing woman be from another world rather than a dream? Crap. The psychic was right. I'd hoped Madame L. was wrong. Way wrong. I waited to hear more before telling Chastity about my previous night. Her information hit me as too strange.

"So if I thought about, say, Mars, I could be there?"

Chastity wrinkled her forehead before answering. "Theoretically, yes."

"Theoretically."

"Yes. It's like dialing into a radio station, but it takes practice."

I shook my head. Too bizarre. "Uh, you'll need to clarify."

"When you're awake during the day, you're dialed in to this life."

"Well, see? I'm off beam. I want the dial position where I'm a successful business owner instead of the working a dead end job with a jerk boss number." I snapped my fingers. "I know. Beam me up, Scotty but check the coordinates first. Right?"

My friend huffed a breath. "No need to get snippy. I'm trying to explain a difficult concept. Give me a break."

My hand enclosed Chastity's wrist lightly. "I'm sorry. You know I don't like this stuff. Why can't you be the one facing this problem?" The unsaid "why me?" echoed in the room.

"It's your lesson."

I shrugged and sighed. "Okay, Teach. I'll try to keep up."

"Do that."

Chastity's uncharacteristically testy reply encouraged my compliance.

"Do you know anything about lucid dreaming?"

"Uh, no."

Chastity tapped her fingernail against the book she held on her lap. "It's a good tool." Leaning forward she said, "Dreams are as real as non-dream time. Lucid dreaming can help you control your dreams, change outcomes."

Aha. The explanation for disappearing woman. Should I relate my experience to her now or wait?

Chastity's fingers snapped before my face. "Wherever you are come back right now."

"Oh, right. Like I could be transported to the past." I snickered.

"Theoretically, it's possible. Everything exists simultaneously, remember?"

My pulse increased. I sure as hell didn't want to relive, or get stuck in my past. "My brain is fried. How about I buy you dinner?" I pondered the book stack, thinking I'd need more nourishment before wading through the tomes. "You know, for all your work on my behalf."

Plus, filling Chastity in on recent occurrences over dinner seemed easier.

My friend shut the book on her lap. "Sounds *great*. Let's run down to Mancini's. We can get a double-shot espresso for dessert."

I groaned. Good thing tomorrow was Saturday. I had a feeling Chastity wouldn't let me go until I'd passed Metaphysics 101 through 500. For starters.

Lucky me.

We entered our names on Mario's waiting list and settled at the bar. Martinis were being shaken to our specifications and the night looked promising. I'd begun relating my recent experiences when I saw Mr. Calendar walk in the door. My jaw dropped, a development Chastity didn't miss. Her eyebrows rose when Mr. C. and his month-worthy friend sat beside us.

Mr. C.'s dark hair looked damp from a recent shower. I didn't need to think twice to know I'd lick him dry. He wore a black tee tight enough to show off his assets. No Mr. Universe but approachable. Some of those pumped up gym rats scare the crap out of me.

His heat warmed my left side and my thoughts.

"Hi, mind if I join you?"

"You already have, but thanks for asking, I guess." Criminy, why did I sound so stupid around this man? And why did I care when I already had a boyfriend?

"Whoa. I can move back beside my friend Mike, but then we'd be at odd ends. I hoped we could keep each other company."

I looked to my right. Chastity was engrossed with the aforementioned Mike. Meeting new guys usually left me tongue-tied. I already felt comfortable enough to smart off with this guy. Though it'd probably be wise to learn his name.

I swung back to him. "My name is Gabriella, but most folks call me Gabby."

"Which name do you prefer? I like Gabriella, myself. It seems to suit you."

"I'll answer to either, but I'm curious."

He tilted his head. "About?"

I smiled. "Well, your name for one. I told you mine."

He held out his hand. A pleasant tingling sensation enveloped my fingers.

"Adrian. Adrian Comstock."

I felt the blood leave my head. Holy Nomenclature. Couldn't be. Dark hair and a name with *both* an A and a C? Well, I guess Madame L had been reading the ethers using lower case. The shapes were similar that way.

"Did I say something wrong?"

"No, not at all." I dredged up a smile. "We seem to be running into each other lately. The Ground Up this morning, now here."

"Yeah, we're fated to meet."

Oh, no. He had to be joking.

"You know, like a planet and a moon in orbit with

each other." He winced. "Didn't sound the way I meant. I should confess right now, I'm a geek. I have no clue about talking with gorgeous women."

I laughed. "I think you've aced the opening, but don't push your luck. Blocking coffee house doors won't always work."

His expression grew solemn. "If I recall correctly, you were the one keeping me from getting past. Did you plan the move?" He rubbed the nape of his neck. "Because you know, it worked. I sure as hell noticed your hair. Well, other parts, too, but mostly your hair."

"I wanted coffee, not a man to waylay." I changed the subject before we dug ourselves a hole we couldn't fill. "Do you come here often?" I winced then laughed. "Maybe you don't remember, but you and Mike sat next to my boyfriend and me here the other night."

"Oh, I remember all right." Adrian frowned. "Your boyfriend? He's not...never mind."

I mentally squirmed and shifted gears yet again. "So are you and Mike roommates?"

Adrian grabbed peanuts from the bowl before me. I pushed it closer to him. The way his arm brushed mine when he'd made the move had created more tingles. Tingles I shouldn't be feeling for a man other than Joel, regardless of the psychic's prediction.

"Nah. Business partners." He sipped his beer. "Computer programs. We met our deadline with twenty minutes to spare, so we're in here celebrating."

He grabbed more peanuts and nodded toward Chastity. "You and your friend? Roommates?"

"Nah," I said, copying his tone. "Neighbors. Friends."

He nodded. "Friends are good."

We sipped and nibbled quietly. My thoughts raced, looking for a way to keep this conversation going, even though I felt like I betrayed Joel. Unfortunately, Adrian wasn't the only nerd inhabiting a bar stool in Mancini's. I proved the supposition with my next words.

"I'm surprised you noticed me at The Ground Up because usually I'm the one who remembers other people," I said. "I have a good memory for faces. I'm always greeting people because they look like friends and then I realize it's the person from the library or someone similar. You know. Not really friends, but acquaintances from the neighborhood. Sorta, kinda." I stuttered to a stop, grabbing my glass like a lifeline.

I gulped. "You probably think I'm an idiot, huh? My mouth opens, words stream out and I can't stop them. It's awful and sometimes I repeat myself. You noticed, huh? I get nervous around really coo…ah, never mind. I'll shut up now." I finished my martini and looked at the bar.

He leaned close and spoke softly at my ear. "Listen, let's pretend we already know each other. Sorta, kinda. Will the pretense be easier for you? And in case you don't remember, because you know so many people, I'm Adrian."

I looked at him from under my lashes and my breath hitched. His eyes gave new meaning to the color brown. They held gold specks and the irises were rimmed with a dark chocolate color. I saw promise there.

"Gabriella," I said and extended my hand to him. Tingles. Again. Maybe the air was filled with static electricity tonight.

"May I buy you a drink?"

"Thanks, but no." I lurched forward as Chastity elbowed me in the ribs. She leaned past me and addressed Adrian.

"Yes, she's delighted with your offer. Don't listen to her. She's shy at inconvenient times." Chastity sent me a stern look. "Take. The. Drink."

I felt my face heat. "I just finished a martini but maybe I'd better switch to the house Chianti, thanks." More than one martini was not smart when faced with a demi-god.

Mario walked up and put his hand on my back. "*Il mio amica*. Would you help me out tonight?"

"Sure. What do you need?"

"I could use a table for two. Would you and your friend mind joining these two gentlemen? You'd be seated much faster."

"We'll take it, Mario," Chastity said. She grinned at me and wiggled her eyebrows. I made a note to get revenge later. Mario clapped Adrian on the shoulder before showing us to a private table in a corner. What the heck?

"I'm sending over a carafe of wine as a thank you," Mario said.

By the time we finished dinner and a second carafe, Mike and Chastity talked with their heads together, oblivious to anyone else. I fought Adrian's tractor beam-like pull, but the more we talked, the faster my resistance sank to a new low. He was funny with nerd factor appeal.

I recalled comments Chastity had made about my appearance, words I'd passed off as ego boosting. Adrian's genuine male interest made me rethink her remarks. He laughed at my silly jokes, and I compared his reactions to Joel's inability to get my humor.

As we left Mancini's, a serious yet basic question hit me. *Did I really want Joel when a demi-god inhabited my sphere? Talk about skanky behavior. Maybe Joel and I hadn't been doing well lately, but we were still a couple. Weren't we?*

My breath caught. My mind reeled. The wine I'd drunk hadn't seemed like much, but could have caused my balance loss. I tripped on a small crack in the sidewalk and Adrian's hand grasped my arm, steadying me. Shoot. I could feel the tingles even though my face felt numb.

We stumbled through the door to my building. I eyed the stairs leading to my top floor apartment. Ordinarily, I had no problem hiking the three long flights, but tonight I thought crawling the best approach. The low, quiet voice at my ear startled me.

"Want help? You can lean on me."

Hmm. Use the wine as an excuse to buddy up with Adrian or crawl and make an even bigger fool of myself? I leaned into his side and felt his arm slip around my waist, anchoring me snugly.

Shit, my vision had messed up. Had to be because a rose-colored tint glowed around the stairs and faded wallpaper in the vestibule. I glanced at Adrian from under my lashes. He carried the same glow. Closing my eyes, I moved my head slightly from side to side against his taut obliques. *The color is gone; the rose tint disappears.*

Opening my eyes, I exhaled my despair. Now gold flakes, like a snowstorm touched by King Midas, swirled in the lobby. A soft voice sounded. *"Go for it, Gabriella. Go upstairs."*

Hallucinations. I saw and heard things but hadn't inhaled anything besides wine.

Our bodies melded. We fit even though he hit six feet and I stand a short inch above petite. Warmth flowed from him. I wanted him in entirety. "I'm on the top floor."

"If you get tired, I'll carry you," he said.

Now I knew I hallucinated. Someone slipped magic mushrooms into the marinara sauce. I extended my foot and felt him half-lift me onto the first step. We moved upstairs.

Chastity and Mike entered the apartment next door as we stepped onto the landing. They hadn't wasted any time. I hiccupped. Yep, I'd had too much wine.

Once inside my home, my nerves attacked, leaving me with a lurching stomach and sweaty palms. I needed a moment alone to think. Would this night end with a new friend, or a man I'd have to avoid every time I went to the store? My brain fuzz meant a decision would take more than a minute, and the increased colors I saw around everything didn't help.

I trotted out my manners. "Make yourself at home. I think I have wine in the fridge."

"I've had enough, thanks." The corners of his mouth rose. "I don't bite." His voiced lowered. "At least not on the first date."

Had I misheard or did he think we were on a date? My face grew warm. "Um, okay. Be right back." I stumbled to my bedroom and sank onto my bed fighting the whirlies.

Flirting with a guy was one thing. Inviting him to my apartment something else. I didn't really know Adrian. Sure, I'd seen him at The Ground Up and

Mancini's. Coincidence. Gorgeous, yes, but he couldn't be interested. He probably wanted to ensure I got home safely. Nothing more.

I mused the date question in the manner of people who have over-imbibed. I remembered his casual touches, the way his eyes darkened when he looked at me, and his husky voice in my ear. If I didn't know better, I'd think he was hitting on me.

I yawned. *Nah, no way. I'll brush my teeth and show him out.* I yawned again. *In a minute.*

Chapter Six

I jerked upright. Whaa?? Someone pounded on my door at——I checked my clock—two a.m.? My heart pounded. Had something happened to Chastity? I sniffed. No smoke smell, thank god.

Running for the door, I narrowly avoided a large pair of feet and stopped mid-stride. Feet? Looking back at the couch, my jaw dropped and my pulse shot into overdrive. Adrian half-sprawled half-sat on my couch. Even in sleep, he looked exhausted. Oh, right. He'd told me he and Mike had been working fifteen hour days. Cyrano was spread along the couch back, looking like a sphinx.

Pounding resumed against my door. "Gab, I know you're in there. Answer the damn door."

Joel. Why the hell did he pick tonight to show after the bars closed? Wait. This could be a strange dream. I glanced back at Adrian. Anyone else would have woken by now. Still a small percentage, the rare chance this really happened, existed. To be on the safe side, I leaned against the door and whispered.

"Joel? It's two o'clock in the morning. I was asleep." My voice held an angry undertone.

"Open the door, Gab. I don't want to wake your pissy neighbor."

Meaning Chastity. He knew she'd call the cops on him and stand in the hall smiling and waving when they came to eject him from the building. I flipped the three locks open and before the final one had fully released, Joel pushed past.

He threw a quick glance and gesture toward Adrian, who struggled awake. "What the shit is this?"

I knew with a soul deep certainty Chastity would celebrate that he'd arrived only because someone had seen me with Adrian and reported back. Cyrano seconded my opinion by arching his back and hissing. I had a sense of him surrounded with an ugly green, and you know the saying about jealousy and green.

Joel crossed his arms. "You're two-timing me?"

He sounded incredulous and I wondered if it was because he thought I couldn't get a man besides him. I felt my anger simmer under the immediate emotional hurt.

"After all I've done for you, this is how I'm repaid?"

A low snarl sounded from the area of the couch, and it didn't come from Cyrano, who now sat at my feet. I froze. The scene seemed unreal.

Adrian unfolded and moved beside me. Heat radiated off him. Nope. Probably not a dream—I hadn't gotten a physical reading from the woman the other night. I watched as his chest puffed out and his muscles grew before my eyes.

"You want to get into it right now? Then let's go outside," Adrian said. "Gabriella doesn't need to see this, you stupid bastard."

Joel added his muscles into the posturing mix and they traded baleful stares.

I took deep breaths, wishing I had a paper bag to blow into. Adrian put his hand on my arm, his voice gentle. "You all right?"

I nodded and heard my voice squeak an unidentifiable word. Clearing my throat, I pointed my finger at Joel. "I don't know who told you what, but nothing is going on here. We both fell asleep, in different rooms, after having dinner. It wasn't pre-planned. We're friends."

Then I turned and pointed at Adrian. "Friends."

Facing Joel again, I put my hands on my hips. "I don't appreciate the way you pushed in here, smelling like a brewery, accusing me of something I would never do. I'm loyal, even to people who treat me like a freaking door mat."

Adrian gave a small cheer under his breath. Joel shifted on his feet.

"Shut up, Adrian, I'm handling this." Surprise colored the realization that I'd stood up for myself. Adrenaline surged through me.

"I want you both to leave." Their expressions of denial registered but my mind had set along with my jaw. "I mean it. After you leave I'm opening the windows to air out the testosterone stink in here."

Neither man moved. I sighed. They acted like two year olds, both wearing firefighter hats and arguing over the lone red truck.

"Adrian, please go."

Joel gloated and looked ready to taunt. I held my hand palm out at my so-called boyfriend.

"Please. I'll be fine." Adrian looked ready for argument, then shook his head and shouldered past Joel.

Joel stalked close and rubbed my upper arms. "Honey, I worried when Bobby told me he'd seen you drunk, walking with some strange dude. I don't want some asshole taking advantage of you."

My skin crawled under his hands, the friction raising uncomfortable goose bumps. Then his words registered. "Don't you mean some asshole besides you? Someone who comes over for meals and never reciprocates? Who expects me to be around when he wants me?"

He stepped back, his eyes narrowing. His low-voiced answer held an underlying threat. "What do you mean?"

His muscles rippled, his jaw clenched and I was happy his aura had dissipated. I suspected it'd be black. My recent bravado evaporated and I dropped my hands from my hips. "Never mind. I'm tired. I want you to leave." Cyrano added an arched back hiss to my request.

A variety of expressions crossed his face then he relaxed and smiled. "Come on, Gab, I came over to check that you're safe."

I doubt it. The thought made me bite back my automatic attempt to placate him. "You have to leave."

The scene left me exhausted. I only wanted sleep. Peaceful, dreamless, uninterrupted.

"Listen, I'm sorry." His voice seemed softer, closer to the way he'd spoken when first we met. He ran his hand through his hair then rubbed his chin. "I guess being without a job is bugging me." He crossed his arms. "I'll give you a call, okay?"

Cyrano pushed against my legs. My shoulders dropped. Being without a job sucked, as I knew first hand, but no excuses. "Not too soon. I need time to think. Now go."

He slipped out the door, closing it softly behind

him. I rubbed my throbbing forehead and temples, got up and set the locks. Resting my forehead against the wood, I gulped down the tears collecting at the back of my throat. How could I move around in other dimensions when I couldn't even handle this one?

I yawned and stumbled into the bathroom. I glanced into the mirror above the sink expecting to see death warmed over. Instead, my eyes looked deeper, wider, and the normal hazel had changed to brown with additional golden specks and a hint of butterscotch amber.

Leaning forward, a fleeting movement crossed my face and superimposed a different, more resolute visage. My eyes were kohl rimmed, I wore a headdress and I had a light brown complexion. Egyptian. I caught the impression of determination and strength along with something alien. It was my face and it wasn't. My eyes held an ageless expression.

I backed up, my hand encircling my throat. Reaching behind me, I flicked off the light and backed out the door. Hanging like a mist in the bathroom was the same bluish-white light I'd seen earlier this week but without the low hum. I whirled, ran for my bed, and threw the covers up over my head. Hugging myself, I curled into a tight fetal position. I felt Cyrano's familiar weight settle at my feet.

Crap. What the hell just happened? I'd better get through Metaphysical 101, fast.

****

"What went on in here last night?" Chastity settled onto the couch.

My friend's early morning appearance was no less attractive for a lack of make-up. I thought I'd come to terms with her beauty, but sometimes after a restless night, I viewed her looks as unfair.

"Adrian and I fell asleep then Joel showed up."

My neighbor's face brightened. I felt like holding my hand before my eyes to keep from being blinded. Sheesh. Grumpy didn't come near to describing my mood today. Having only myself to blame bit my ass.

"Don't get all excited. He flopped on the couch and I passed out in bed. We were both dressed." The story of my life. Lately I got less sex than a practicing celibate.

The disappointment on my friend's face would be comical if I were in a good mood.

"However," Chastity's face lit up again, with the word, "you'll be happy to hear I told them both to leave."

"Why should I be happy?" A brief wrinkle passed across her forehead. "Oh, you kicked Joel out? Good for you."

I hesitated, wondering how to explain what I'd seen in the mirror.

Chastity interrupted my internal debate. "Don't you want to know what happened next door?"

I mustered a smile morphing to genuine when I saw the flustered, excited look on her face. For all her beauty, my neighbor didn't date, or at least didn't invite a guy home the first night they met. Time to move into listener mode. "Woo-hoo, cutie. Did you get some?"

"We *talked.*"

I examined my fingernails to hide my smile. "Ah huh, sure."

"Gabriella, I think he may be *The One*."

Sitting up straight, I leaned forward, supporting my

upper body with my hands. "No way."

"Yes *way*."

I sat back, oddly deflated with the news. My best friend had found a sweet man. When Mike called her—because there was no question he would—they'd start dating. Then spend all their time as a couple, moving in together soon after. And I'd still be sitting here. Alone. Shoot. I didn't even remember Mike's last name.

As much as I wanted only the best for my friend, after last night I knew my time with Joel was limited. How could Chastity and I compare happy notes if one of us was miserable? Dang, I needed to grow up. My best friend deserved a sweet guy and I'd cheer her on.

Her strong grip enveloped my hand. "Don't go there."

I blinked. "Huh?"

"Stop thinking you'll be alone and I won't have time for you anymore. You're my BFF." She grinned. "And Mike's last name is Jarvis."

How did she know I couldn't remember his name? Oh, right. She knows me. I didn't want to admit my friend was right about my worries or go into details so I misled her. "Actually, I'm thinking my time with Joel is ending."

"I hope Adrian is on your to-date short list."

I snorted. "Right, like he's interested after I insisted he leave." I ducked my head, my friend's expression sending a bolt of guilt through me. "Okay, okay," I muttered. "I screwed up."

Chastity opened her mouth then closed it without speaking and shook her head slowly. Her measured glance left me feeling scolded yet silence had reigned.

My neighbor pointed to the stack on the floor.

"Let's get to work. We have way too much to cover, and I get the feeling things are breaking loose."

"Crap. I haven't told you about the disappearing woman or what I saw in the mirror." I related both stories. I cocked my head, waiting for her verdict.

"Taking initiative, telling both men to leave, probably brought back a lifetime memory when you were in charge. The other vision, disappearing woman, could be a message from your higher self, a taste of your potential if you follow your dreams. Or it could be you in a different dimension. Either way, there's no time to lose." She grabbed the top book and flipped through pages. "Alternate universes. No, parallel universes. Where did I see the reference?"

Shi—oot. I swallowed past a dry lump blocking my throat. This didn't sound good.

"Here it is." Long fingers smoothed down a page; one hand reached to flick back silky blond hair. "This study says an object you see before you can also exist simultaneously in a parallel universe." Her emerald green gaze caught mine. "I think it a likely explanation for disappearing woman. You saw yourself in an alternate life."

My throat closed, my breath seized. The explanation filled me with a sense of rightness and explained why the woman looked familiar. I fell back against the cushions. Holy Time Traveler. In an alternate place, I dated Adrian. Sweet Creamy Cannoli. The other me not only had money and good taste, but a sexy and caring boyfriend.

"Remember what I said about dialing in to a time?"

I nodded a head three sizes too big and fuzzy. I remembered, didn't I?

"This study says when you watch something in one state, it gets split somehow. The split off portion is in a different place from the watcher. So there are multiple universes but we only see one at a time."

I held up a hand, palm out. "Sorry." Man, my voice sounded like a squeaky gate. I cleared my throat and began again. "You lost me. Are you saying there are two of me?"

My friend nodded. "Yep. Maybe more. Every time you make a decision, a life-altering choice, you create a timeline. For example, when you break with Joel, one path will be created where you have a life without him. The other path continues onward as if you hadn't split up."

"And this happens with each big choice, like pursuing one career field over another?"

"Yes, a big probability."

"Dang." I thought for a moment. "Do you think you're in all my lives?"

My friend shrugged, not the answer I wanted.

"So I can really go back to the future?"

Chastity placed her forefinger against her mouth and her eyes studied the ceiling. "You weren't listening, were you?"

I gulped. "Um."

"This is important. All time happens at once. There's no linear time track to follow. Particles travel both forward and backward in time. Maybe time zigzags. Hard to say."

I needed a guide and Chastity seemed to be abdicating. Where was Tonto when Kemo Sabe needed him? And why was the Lone Ranger referred to as "Trusty Scout" when Tonto did all the tracking?

Actually, Mr. Spock's cool deliberation would be handy. If anyone could navigate weird time stuff, it would be a Vulcan.

My friend's voice pulled my wayward attention back from fictional heroes. "Gabriella, there's no telling what will happen to you."

Nonono. Not the words I wanted to hear.

Chapter Seven

I clattered down warped wooden stairs and entered my favorite bookstore. Up On Books inhabited the basement of a building built into a hillside. I loved the business name's play on words almost as much as I did the store's owner.

Leonard was a throwback to an earlier era. Today he'd encased his lanky frame in a white shirt, string tie, black dress slacks, and shiny black shoes. His wiry gray hair had been trimmed into a short brush cut.

Besides owning the shop, he played in a jazz trio on weekends. He said popular music had turned to trash after the Korean War, and believed his weakness for Motown remained a secret. I knew better and teased him by variously referring to him as Otis, Wilson, and Al, for Redding, Pickett, and Green.

"Hey, Otis."

"Good morning, Miss Gabriella. Once again, I ask that you refer to me as Leonard."

I held back a smile. "Leonard, do you have any books on quantum mechanics?"

"Your Miss Chastity came in here yesterday and cleaned me out." He squinted. "Are you two planning a time machine?"

I winced. "It's um, a gift."

He snorted. "You should work on your prevarication skills my young friend."

I opened my eyes wide. "Me?"

He shook his head and shuffled around the counter. Heading down an aisle marked "Non-fiction and Poetry," he ran agile fingers along the shelves, stopping halfway along the row. He pulled out a thin volume.

"This came in after Chastity left. Don't know why, but I thought of you."

Muttering a curse under my breath, I turned the book over. My head shot up along with my blood pressure. "Leonard. What the freaking hell is this? *Time Travel, Conspiracy Theories, and UFOs*?"

He shook a finger in my face. "Missy, watch your language. If you can't express yourself without using scatological references, buy a dictionary." He grumbled quietly while walking toward the counter.

I inhaled several times in a vain attempt to lower my pulse rate. Damn it all to hell. It seemed everyone I knew connived to involve me with woo-woo crap. And clean language.

I tried to re-shelve the UFO book, but the space remained jam-packed. The book itself seemed glued to my hand. I exhaled in a huff. May as well look at the damn thing.

Although the book looked new, an anomaly to this store, it opened directly to a page headed, 'Nuclear Missile Crisis: All Blown Up?' I sank to the floor, leaned against the shelves and browsed.

Sometime later, I raised my head, sure my eyes had glazed over. I probably resembled Snow White's Dopey, and with good reason. If this author spoke truth, history consisted of smoke and mirrors. World events were influenced by E.T.s. Up was down and time zigzagged. Or maybe not. I sighed.

My life looked more like a screwed up mess every minute. The book confirmed colors and low hums could precede dimension changes. Oh, crap.

I bought the book, tucked it under my arm, and left. As I topped the stairs, the floor shook slightly, accompanied by the strange feeling you get when an earthquake rumbles, a sensation that the normal fabric of existence has been slit by a fingernail. I made sure I had my balance and stepped outside.

Bright sunlight glared off a parked car's hood in front of the bookstore entrance, causing a combined prism and halo effect. A bluish light rimmed the halo. The street noise faded into a low hum. Rubbing my eyes, I took a step and stopped. Instead of the cracked sidewalk I knew fronted the doorway, I saw dirt.

Lifting my head, I saw a scene in faint overlay, a picture from the past. A pen filled with cows kicking up dust had appeared across the street. Four men sat playing cards in the shade thrown by fence slats. Two others leaned against a tree trunk, their hats tipped forward over their faces, a dog resting at their feet.

I stood still. This couldn't be an acid flashback because I'd never used a hallucinogen, leaving one obvious explanation. Hang over. The worst hang over of all time. Nope, I'd recovered from last night. Unless I'd seen re-enactors. That's what they were.

Or the worst truth—time had shifted and I'd moved between worlds.

I turned and ran back downstairs, happy to note the bookstore remained in place. "Leonard, did Harteville ever have cattle drives, with you know, cowboys?"

He stared at me, not answering. I patted myself down craning to look behind me. All my body parts remained in place.

He blinked. "What's wrong, Miss Gabriella?"

I quickly surveyed my appearance. "What do you mean?"

He pursed his lips. "You called me Leonard and your face is whiter than tapioca."

Euww. Pudding face. Lovely. "Never mind about my face. Do you know local history?"

"As a matter of fact, I do."

My chest loosened. Finally, I'd get answers.

"Do you know if this was a cattle town? You know, like a place where cows were corralled? A round-up place?"

He stared at me as if trying to decide how much to say, or perhaps wondering why I didn't know local lore. "You're familiar with the Buncombe Turnpike through Asheville? Farmers in Tennessee drove their livestock along the Turnpike to reach Atlanta and Charleston markets. Hartesville was founded alongside one of that route's offshoots. We didn't see the same business level as the inns along the Turnpike, but we got our share."

"So this area was a highway of sorts."

"That's correct. How do you feel? Your face has lost the little color it had."

"Mmrph."

I climbed the stairs, grabbed the knob and pushed open the door. Sticking my head out, I faced a normal neighborhood scene. No cattle, no men, no dust devils, no low humming sound. Only my own mental demons informing me that if I kept seeing things, I'd better not tell anyone besides Chastity. Straight jackets weren't in season this fall.

****

I walked slowly carrying the book under my arm. As I swung onto the street leading home, I noticed Adrian emerging from a stairwell, smoothing back his hair. I crossed the street and headed his way. He leaned against the banister, evidently awaiting my approach.

"Hey, Gabby. How goes it today?" He winced.

I hoped the wince indicated he'd meant to sound more suave than inane.

"Fine. Just…fine." Shoot, now I sounded like an idiot. Nothing new around this guy.

He straightened, his hand on my shoulder faster than I knew a human could move.

"What is it? What's wrong? Is someone causing you a problem?" He dropped his hand and stepped away.

Hell, we'd never even dated and he acted as if he cared. My face muscles formed a tentative smile. "I'm trying to work out a sort of problem. I had the strangest thing happen a little bit ago."

He waited, but I'd stopped speaking and stood with my head down. I hadn't meant to talk about my experience with anyone but Chastity. How could I back out now?

"Gabriella? May I help you?"

My head moved in a "no" motion before I looked up. "Thanks anyway."

He dropped onto a stair and motioned to the space beside him. I sat, but not close. On the same stair, but the gap between us was more than physical.

"Want to tell me your problem?"

Sudden heat spread from my hair roots to my neck, where it disappeared under my sweater. I tried on a smile, hoping it didn't resemble a death mask. "Um, no.

I'm a mess."

"Being a problem solver by nature, I like messes." His upper body leaned toward mine. "Um, I'm taking a work break. How about I walk you home." He stood, ducked his head, and shuffled his feet. "Carry your books for you, little girl?"

"My Mom told me to never speak with strangers."

"I'm not offering you candy, only companionship." He held out a hand to help me up. "Plus, we had dinner together last night." His hand tightened around mine.

"Yes, well I apologize for the scene later. Joel is, um, well he—"

"Words can't describe him, I know. Let's leave it." He reached for the book I carried and read the title aloud. His eyebrows rose. "I'd never have pegged you for a conspiracy theorist."

My face heated again, or maybe still. "A friend recommended the book, but I probably won't read the thing. It's over my head."

His reply sounded intense. "Stop it. You need to stop tearing yourself down."

I stared at him then pulled my arm from his grasp. "What are you, my high school guidance counselor?"

He stepped back. "No! No, I mean you have a lot going for you and I think—" Taking a deep breath, he began again. "Look, I think you're, you know. Special." His expression looked like he'd stepped in horse dung.

I glanced over the street but the scene appeared real time so I pinched myself, leaving a white mark behind. No dream, but totally inappropriate for my pulse to jump given I hadn't squared things with Joel, yet.

"I, um, gotta run. Nice seeing you again." I turned from him and took two steps but could hear his mutter.

"I should stick to writing code," Adrian said. "At least in the computer games, I always get the girl."

****

"So there I was, watching a live scene from a John Wayne movie. Or maybe Daniel Boone. History isn't my thing. What do you think?" I sat forward, eager for Chastity's response.

"Whoa. You're moving, girlfriend. Remote viewing, maybe. Way remote."

"Thanks, Good Witch Glenda. I wonder where I'll end up."

"With me, if here is where you put your concentration." Chastity sank down beside me on the couch and gave me a long look. "Stop acting the victim. You've got control over your life."

"What do you mean?"

"I believe every major choice made creates an echo in time."

"You mean besides the main choices causing separate lives?" I shook my head. "Easy for you to say."

"Easy for you to *do*, if you want. Listen, we've talked about this before. Bad choices can be turned around with good ones. Your subconscious knows what's stopping you from living the life you deserve. I can't tell you. Listen to your higher self and *pay attention*. If you don't embrace this project and make it your own, you'll be like flotsam in the sea of life."

"A pretty simile, Chastity. Did you lift it from a commercial or have you been sneaking Oprah again?"

"Don't even try changing the subject, Gabriella. This is serious." She tilted her head to the side. "I won't say more on the subject because you've decided to

65

learn this the hard way. Goddess Bless."

A cold shiver slid down my spine. If I believed in premonitions, I'd think an omen had chilled me.

My neighbor's gaze was warm and sympathetic and scared me crapless. "Sweetie. One day you'll have to stop denying the truth."

"I'd hoped I could avoid thinking until maybe death."

Chastity patted my hand. "I get it." She returned her attention to the book. "Now where did I read about worm holes?" She put the volume aside and bent to scavenge through the stacks. Picking up a red covered tome, she opened to the book's middle pages.

"We're going fishing?"

My friend looked up with a smile. "I'm referring to inter-galactic travel but wormholes can be dimensional."

"Yikes."

"I don't think you'll be leaving Earth, but forewarned is…you know."

I chewed my thumbnail.

"Gabriella, you'll be fine, I promise."

"Oh, so you'll accompany me when I wig out?"

"You can never tell. I've learned some things over…over the course of my research. I'm looking for a way to help you, to travel with you, when you go."

I knew my eyes narrowed. "Don't mess with me."

"I'm not. I've got some things to work out and I can't guarantee anything, but I'll do my best."

I opened my mouth to ask a probing question, my nerves on edge and my brain clamoring for answers. My neighbor forestalled me by picking up a book and jumping into a monologue.

Chastity wouldn't escape easily. She knew more than she was saying. She'd sent me to Madame LaMere, a woman who conveniently disappeared after we spoke. She knew where to look for books holding needed answers. More happened inside her blonde head than anyone knew. Something stunk, and it wasn't the rustic goat cheese manufacturer on the other side of the river, or even the micro-breweries. The odor lay heavy in this very room.

We kept to our studies taking a break for dinner, which we ate in with Cyrano for company. I hadn't heard from Joel even though it was a date night. No surprise given the banishment I'd laid on him. He had never been the most assiduous man I'd dated, just one of the few. He'd said he'd call me, and I was pleased he'd paid attention when I asked for time to think. I'd be even more relieved if he'd go away and never contact me again. Yeah, I tend to take the coward's way out whenever possible.

However, Joel played a dual role, giving me time to decide what to do about the puzzle piece Adrian represented. I still wasn't sure I could trust his apparent interest, though I enjoyed the heck out of being with the man. Good-looking, intelligent, funny, generous—what wasn't to like? An uneasy flicker, one whose origin I couldn't determine, belied he could be totally trusted.

Or perhaps I couldn't trust myself to trust a man.

At ten, Chastity stretched. "I'm done. Mike and I are going clubbing. He'll be here in an hour."

I stretched my neck, jumping when a bone popped back into place. "Thanks again for doing the research." I rubbed my eyes. "More, for being here and helping me make sense of this stuff. If you hadn't explained what was happening, I'd be overmedicated in a hospital. Or sitting in a jail cell."

She laughed. "No you wouldn't. You may have opened one too many wine bottles to dull your senses, but give yourself credit. You'd have found your way to the information." She extended her arms over her head and went up on tiptoe. "I'm happy to help."

We said goodnight and I locked my door after watching Chastity enter her apartment. I considered making coffee. Given what I'd seen the last two nights, I wasn't sure I wanted to drift into dreamland. My body had other plans, and before long, the combination of a warm cat on my lap and too much reading made my eyelids droop.

The dream began as a series of disjointed pictures. Girls in gingham dresses, horses in a pasture, a one-story clapboard house, and rounded mountains in the distance flipped past like flash cards. The quick sequence ended on what appeared to be a pioneer town's main street. I didn't notice smells, but knew the street was dusty. Dry as a desiccant.

In the way of dreams, I spoke with a man who stood behind a counter in a general store. Small windows allowed a modicum of light to enter the dusky space. The wall shelves were packed floor to ceiling, and a rolling ladder stood close by to access products stored higher up. Large jars of candy were placed next to the register, with wooden cases of vegetables and a large pickle barrel nearby.

Goods I planned to purchase were piled up between us. He chattered, but I didn't really pay attention to his words. Instead, I was anxious I'd taken too long. The person waiting for me didn't have patience.

Next, I approached a wagon hitched with two brown horses. I "knew" I tended the animals, and their soft nickering as I drew close supported my impression. Although I wanted to stop and nuzzle them, I felt pressured for time.

A male sat on the buckboard with his hat pulled low shading his face. I suspected I had a connection to the man, but I couldn't see his face. He projected an air of controlled anger, or perhaps danger.

The store clerk threw two large bags onto the buckboard, and the resulting white cloud told me they were filled with flour. He went into the store and returned with several more large burlap bags. Corn. Beans. Finally, he returned with two wooden boxes loaded with twine-wrapped packages. The clerk handed the small packets to me, nodded, then left.

My long skirts swirled around my legs as I lifted my smaller packages onto the wagon bench.

"Hurry it up, sis. Ain't got all day."

Sis? Then this was my brother? His voice struck a chord, but I still couldn't see his face. Although in present time I'd struggle to climb into a large SUV, my dream persona had no problem clambering onto the seat, even in long skirts and petticoats.

A man on horseback appeared and my dream brother stiffened. "God damn, hurry up. We gotta move." Settled on the bench, I finally glimpsed the driver's face. Although he sported a beard and stringy brown hair, his eyes were Joel's.

The horse and rider halted next to the wagon.

Joel spat over the wagon's side. "Sheriff."

My lungs seized. Dark hair. High cheekbones. Tan

skin. Too familiar eyes. *Adrian.*

He nodded at my brother. "Jebediah." Two fingers went to his hat brim in a courteous salute. "Miss Genevieve."

"Sheriff Adam." My dream persona answered with a small smile.

The two men eyed each other like long-term antagonists. The clues were in their stiff body language and stilted language, like two strange dogs meeting at the green space down the street. If these guys were dogs, they needed to wag more and bark less.

"I told you to leave my sister alone, *Sheriff.*"

"I'm merely being polite."

"Be polite somewhere else."

Gasping, I sat upright, my heart pounding as the dream's ending refrain echoed. I sank against my pillows, trying to regulate my breaths. Thanks to Chastity's tutoring, I understood souls took turns playing out different roles. A mother in one life could be a brother to her former son in the next. Souls switched gender as easily as rich women collected expensive shoes. Still, I hadn't expected to dream of Joel as a brother. The idea made my skin crawl.

He was my brother back then but not a loving sibling. My loyalty toward him made more sense, and I contemplated the other roles we could have played for each other over our shared lives. What else did we need to heal in this lifetime?

Adrian as sheriff? Figured.

I rubbed my chest, hoping the action would slow my pulse. Flipping on a small lamp, I grabbed a notebook and pen, and recorded as many dream details as I could remember. Then I lay on my back staring at the ceiling until the sky lightened outside my window.

Stumbling into the kitchen, I fired up the coffeemaker and slid into a nearby chair.

What a freaky dream. My left brain wouldn't stop spinning scenarios, trying to make sense of the nonsensical.

I wished I could call Chastity, but she'd still be sleeping off her clubbing date with Mike. I pushed a mug under the brewing coffee, replaced the pot, and curled up on my couch. Although Chastity would support me through whatever was destined, I knew I'd have to develop a backbone. I may as well suck up and try figuring this crap out.

The mug warmed my icy fingers and the coffee I sipped gave me a sense of control, or perhaps false courage. If my friend were right, I could take charge of what happened next. Yeah, I liked the idea. Living like a refugee no longer appealed.

My gaze took in the dingy walls, multiple nail holes left by former tenants, and worn furniture. My budget didn't hold much leeway, but I could spring for spackle and paint. Maybe I could even get the landlord to give me a break on the rent for my work. I snorted at the idea then caught myself. Time to start creating the future I wanted.

My right brain took over and began considering colors. Nothing I imagined clicked with my sofa until I remembered a colorful throw I'd bought last month then stored in the closet. Joel had said the pattern reminded him of a restaurant's dumpster contents.

I dug through the closet and pulled the throw from a plastic bag. After arranging the cotton material over the sofa, several color combinations became clear. Now

I had a multitude of choices rather than none. I'd buy the paint today. And the throw would remain. If Joel said anything, I'd tell him to pay my rent.

My decisions left me feeling empowered. The sun had risen and the morning beckoned. I threw on my exercise clothes and clattered outside.

Thirty minutes later I limped around the corner, my hair plastered to my head. My lungs heaved. Swallowing would have eased my throat if I'd had the capacity to generate saliva. Why the heck had I broken into a jog? I'd let my I'm-taking-control-of-my-life-enthusiasm get way out of hand, and now I'd pay the astronomical price.

Adding insult to freaking injury, Adrian left his building half a block down and moved into a smooth jog, underscoring his athleticism. His pace picked up after our glances met. Figured I'd met Mr. Demi-god before my shower and toothbrush.

He slid to a stop. "Good morning."

I brushed my hand over my mouth as I answered. "Morning."

"I noticed you were limping. Did you pull a muscle? Do you need help climbing your stairs? Or I can rub your leg for you."

Shaking my head, I clamped my arms against my body. Had I bothered using deodorant before leaving on my ill-fated early morning jaunt?

His forehead wrinkled. Dang. Even confusion looked good on him.

"You sure you're okay?"

Nodding, I shifted from foot to foot. "Yep," I said through clenched teeth. I hoped I hadn't exhaled on the Harteville heartthrob.

He copied my shifting gesture. "Okay, then I'm off. See you later? I'm meeting Mike and Chastity at The Pastry Oven for brunch at eleven."

I rubbed my jaw as if in thought. "Sure," I replied past my fingers.

"Great! See you there." He half saluted and accelerated into a smooth pace.

I watched him leave, the rear view almost better than his front. Naturally, he looked over his shoulder and caught me gaping. He turned and jogged back.

He ran his fingers through his hair. "Look, you'll probably think I'm sticking my nose in, but I really wanna know. Is there any chance we can move past Friday night? Even though I think your boyfriend's a douche, he's your choice. I'm hoping we can be friends."

I said the first thing leaping to mind. "Why?"

"Why?" He looked stumped. He shook his head slowly. "Because you deserve friends who care about you and who treat you well. People like Chastity, Mike, and myself."

"Right. Our best friends date, we should get along." My stomach dropped.

"No." He rubbed the nape of his neck. "Look, I can't stop thinking about you. I want to spend time together. I'd like to know if I have a chance or if I should walk away. Simple."

Simple? Uh uh. Our gazes met and held. I felt as if I'd dropped into a kaleidoscope pattern until a breeze hit my sweat.

"I need...I need a shower. See you at brunch, okay? We can talk then."

He didn't move as I turned and limped inside.

Chapter Eight

Chastity had called twice and stopped by once to ensure I would show for brunch. Sheesh. You'd think she considered me a scaredy cat.

Fine. I admit I was reluctant about breaking with Joel. Truth to tell, she and Madame L. had made such a big deal about healing the past, I wasn't sure I should walk away from Joel. Perhaps we weren't done with each other yet, but dragging my feet didn't help. Although if karma existed, I didn't want another bad relationship break-up on my record.

I shook off those thoughts and concentrated on the clothes Chastity had chosen. The bright pink sundress with splashy white flowers was too summery, but she'd insisted I needed to show off my legs. She'd also scoffed when I maintained Adrian was no more than a new friend. She could be right, but I wasn't traveling that route today.

The other outfit, a denim mini-skirt with matching top, had the casual look I preferred, but paired with the high heels she'd left on the floor, screamed "available for a date." I didn't want to send the wrong message. Okay, I did but not today, and the temptation lurked like a mugger near a dimly lit ATM.

I compromised with a pair of dark capris and the denim top, adding dangly earrings at the last moment. When Chastity and Mike stopped on their way out, she looked me over and gave an approving nod.

All that remained was remembering to breathe and I'd be in business.

Although the colors I'd seen around the trees and flowers during my aborted jog this morning had seemed sharper and more intense, no odd auras had popped up, even when I'd spoken with Adrian. Unsure whether I should be happy or disgruntled with the lack, I trailed my friends into The Pastry Oven. And walked into the damn bluish light and low-pitched hum.

A modern day Pastry Oven morphed into a tearoom filled with soldiers and their lady friends. No problem except the uniforms were Confederate, and the women spoke with soft Southern drawls. Holy Lace and Cotton Drawers.

Chastity grabbed me by the arm and, saying something to Mike about putting his name on the waiting list, steered me back outside. Where cars and modern life ruled.

"What happened back there? You looked ready to faint."

"You didn't tell me to dress for a *Gone With the Wind* theater party."

She looked at the door. "No one inside is dressed in old clothes." Her gaze searched mine. "You saw soldiers? Women in long dresses?"

I nodded.

She grasped my hand. "I'm so *sorry*. There must be a dimensional gateway here. We can eat elsewhere."

I glanced at the interior through the café's large front window. "Not a problem. Looks normal now."

Mike emerged from the doorway as Adrian strode up.

Squeezing her hand, I nodded toward the two men. "I'll be fine. Let's stay. If I see something funky, I'll excuse myself. No need to ruin your brunch."

Besides, Adrian's appearance initiated a need to learn more about him.

We'd crammed onto a sidewalk bench outside the restaurant and were laughing at Mike's jokes when the hair on my neck stood up. Tensing, I waited for the blue light and the hum, but neither happened. Instead, a real-time fright began.

Joel approached. Hoping he hadn't spotted me, I scrunched down and searched my handbag. The others hadn't noticed Joel, and I hoped he'd walk by in ignorance.

No such luck.

"Gab?"

I raised my head and met Joel's eyes. "Joel? Hi."

He pointed at Adrian. "So is he why you said not to call? You really are two-timing me with nerd-boy."

His tone made me want to slap him. I stood, blocking Adrian from moving and also from Joel's sight. "I'm having brunch with friends. Would you like to join us? I'm afraid I only have enough money for my own meal, though." I sent a mental command to Chastity, asking she remain quiet.

His eyes narrowed.

"We can change our table request to five, if you want to eat here. I'm sure they can find an extra chair." My telepathic request to Chastity must have worked because she didn't say a word, didn't even grunt or snort.

"I'm on my way to meet a friend or I'd consider staying," he said.

"Maybe next time," Mike said and smiled. "They make a mean waffle stack."

"Yeah, I know," Joel said.

He knew? He'd never brought me here, saying the café was overpriced.

My dismay at being seen giggling with Adrian changed to simmering anger. As if he felt the shift, Adrian placed his palm at the small of my back.

More relaxed, I examined Joel's clothes. He looked as if he were coming home after a late night at the bars. Smelled like stale beer, too. That observation sparked my next words.

"If you aren't doing anything later today, stop by. I'm painting my living room after brunch. You're welcome to come help. Say in two hours?"

"Sorry. I'm hanging with Bobby this afternoon."

"No problem. I'll be masking off and spackling today. I probably won't get to painting until later this week. You can help me after dinner one night."

He shook his head. "Naw, you know I don't like ladders, and paint fumes give me a headache." He moved closer, lowering his voice.

"You know I care about you, Gab, but I'm already booked this afternoon. Can't let Bobby down. He's counting on me. I'll help out more. It'll be better between us."

Joel pulled me into his arms and gave me an extended kiss. I knew the kiss was more about ownership than affection, as I now recognized his promises were lies.

His kiss generated no physical response, instead, I felt used. I pulled away, barely stopping myself from wiping my lips with the back of my hand. My reaction told me more than my thoughts had about my feelings. Too bad I still felt linked to him in some odd manner. As if I owed him allegiance. I'd examine the idea later. Perhaps one of Chastity's "ology" books held an answer.

"If you say so. Bye, Joel."

"I do say so. I'll make everything up to you. I promise." He strode off without a backward glance and I sank onto the bench. Adrian had dropped his palm when Joel pulled me into his embrace. Now he sat stiffly. I scooted to the bench's end, forced my lips to curve upward, and turned to face the others.

"So, I guess I should skip brunch. I really do plan to paint this afternoon, and they still haven't called for us. I'll get going."

The hostess appeared at the door calling, "Mike, party of four."

Chastity grinned and waved to the hostess. "You aren't getting off so easily, my friend."

She grabbed my arm, pulling me to my feet. She hadn't been lying when she said she'd been working out. She put her mouth next to my ear. "You didn't fall for his nice talk, did you?"

"Not here," I whispered back.

She straightened. "While we're eating, you can tell us all about your new project." She steered our group toward the door. "In fact, with these two strong men helping, I bet your painting project wouldn't take long at all."

"Yeah, we don't mind helping," Adrian said. "In fact, it'd be a pleasure."

Once again, he placed his palm at the small of my back. The heat from his hand burned through the denim. Suddenly I had a new picture of him helping me, an R-rated image. I blew out a breath and followed the others as we wound our way through the bustling café. Even a tall glass of ice water wouldn't cool me down fast enough.

Before an hour had passed, I faced three eager painting volunteers.

I laughed. "Hey, you guys, slow down. I haven't even bought the paint yet. Besides, I need rollers and brushes. Oh, and maybe newspapers or a tarp or something for the floor. And masking tape. Shoot, what am I forgetting?"

"A ladder." Adrian placed his hand over mine. "You're forgetting Mike and I told you we're old hands at this. We have the supplies and the know-how. We love paint fumes." He inhaled and thumped his chest. "Grows chest hair."

"I thought hot sauce and horseradish thickened hair?" I tried ignoring his torso. No go.

"Yeah, and paint fumes," Mike said.

"Make sure to buy low VOC and you won't have to sleep with your windows open," Adrian said.

"And I'll come along to help with the color choice," Chastity said. "Won't take long to stop back for your cotton throw, and Mike can drive us while Adrian picks up the tools."

I saluted. "Yes, ma'am."

Adrian grabbed the check and stood. "I'll handle this and meet you at the apartment in forty minutes." He threw down several bills totaling more than a twenty percent tip.

I fumbled for my handbag. "Let me give you what I owe for brunch."

He tensed. "I said I'd take care of the bill." Chastity nudged him. "How about we settle later? Mike and I don't work totally for free, you know. You'll owe us."

My shoulders headed for my ears until I saw him wiggle his eyebrows. "I hope you take IOUs," I replied. "Chastity will vouch for me. I'm good for the cash."

A flurry of activity later, I stood at my open apartment door with a gallon of paint at my feet, a cotton throw in my hands, and Chastity at my side. Adrian hadn't arrived and Mike had gone home to change into his paint clothes.

"You didn't really expect me to paint did you?" she asked. "I'm at my best when I'm directing the action and Mike is a natural at—"

"Yeww." I stuck my fingers in my ears. "Too much information."

"Wimp. Besides, someone must calm Cyrano during the invasion. That'll be my job. Get ready. The guys will arrive any minute."

I changed clothes and was moving breakables into the kitchen area when my helpers knocked. I've long held a belief that only horses and ponies pranced. Chastity proved me wrong as she led Mike and Adrian through the door.

"Hey, I've got soft drinks and snacks," I said. "Kitchen is to your left."

Mike displayed one of Chastity's brightly colored ceramic mugs. A wince flashed across his face. "I'll have tea, thanks."

Oh, excellent. Chastity had a new victim, uh, loved one to detox. I'd have to let him in on the palm tree solution. But maybe not today.

Chastity hadn't joked about directing the action. Before long, furniture had been moved or covered, the paint had been stirred, and color hit the walls. Three hours later, my living room walls shone with new life. She handed me the cotton throw, and in coordinated motions, we covered the couch, adding the final touch to pull the room together.

She put her arm around Mike. "You did good, sweetie." He kissed her forehead.

Once again, I felt loneliness swoop. Chastity and Joel hated each other, so even if I salvaged a relationship with him, we wouldn't be double dating.

Adrian clapped his hands twice. "What say we celebrate a job well done?" He checked his watch. "How about a quick dinner?"

"Sorry, can't tonight," I said. "Though I'm inviting you all to dinner as a thank you for your work today. Say, next Thursday night?"

"Make it Friday and you've got a deal," Adrian said.

"Fine with me," Chastity said. "We can all go clubbing afterward."

Trust my friend to up the ante from a simple thank you meal to an all-night affair. I felt my face heat. "Affair" wasn't the correct word given my complicated romantic situation, but I couldn't help focusing on Adrian's lips while I considered the term.

"Great," Mike chimed in. "We're set for next Friday." He slung his arm over Chastity's shoulders. "Hey, sweet stuff, let me walk you home."

The sexual tension should have diminished after they left, but seemed to grow once Adrian and I were alone. I searched for a low-heat topic to diffuse the atmosphere.

"I'd expect you to have a hot date on Friday night rather than coming here for a meal." Shit. Stupid, stupid, stupid comment.

His dark gaze settled on mine. "I do have a hot date. Now."

The heat in my face inched up the thermometer. "Oh, um." I cleared my throat. "I offered a meal to say thanks, not looking for a night out dancing."

He tilted his head, his gaze tangling with mine. "Look, I can wait until you make a decision about the douche, but I'm really hoping you'll kick him to the curb soon. Until then, don't expect me to hold back."

His palm and fingers cupped my face, and his thumb rested at the corner of my mouth. "Sorry. I can't wait for *this*."

His head lowered and his lips touching mine set off a storm of tingles traveling my spine from top to bottom and back. His lips were soft, his pressure firm, and my pulse picked up. This was no kiss for show. He meant every lick and nip. Holy Osculation.

He pulled back, his forehead resting against mine. Our rapid breaths intermingled. "You've ruined me. Dreaming about kissing you kept me awake for hours. The reality?" His slowly shook his head. "No words."

I gulped. "Yeah. You definitely gave me something to think about."

"Good." He stepped back. "Guess I'd better leave so I don't turn into a liar about waiting for your decision."

Adrian closed the door quietly, after reminding me to lock up after him. Really? My body hummed and the last thing I wanted was his exit. Then my conscience spoke. I shouldn't have listened but I did. And I remembered the early times with Joel.

Not long before I met Joel, Howie had been hired as supervisor rather than J&J promoting Donna, who totally deserved the job and pay increase. An exodus of our close and efficient work team—more family than co-workers—had begun. Howie targeted me, but I'd been smart enough to avoid his obvious traps.

Besides work problems, I hadn't had a date in months, okay two years, and my mom pushed me into a series of blind dates encompassing the most boring men I'd ever met. Then she and dad had packed up and moved away. Yes, I have plenty of other relatives in town and I speak with my folks regularly, but as an only child, I felt bereft. Orphaned. Abandoned by the two people I'd counted on my whole life.

I saw only that my life sucked, not the potential. Suicidal? No. But wounded.

Then I was out with Chastity at a club. Men were falling at her feet—I saw them though they tried to recover with clumsy dance moves—and I sat sipping my wine and waiting to leave. Joel slid onto the bar stool next to mine and struck up a conversation. He was handsome. Funny. Toned and tanned. I figured he knew I was with Chastity and looked for a way to meet her.

But he concentrated on me. All night. As we were leaving, he trapped me against the bar with his arms and teased I couldn't leave without giving him my phone number. The scene replayed against my eyelids as I remembered his sweet smile and earnest expression.

From then on, my life took a major turn. When my parents talked about their new lives, I celebrated their happiness. Howie making snide comments about me at work? I laughed. Rather than being upset because Donna had been passed over, we began planning to start our own businesses.

So even though Joel and I had recently hit a rough spot, he'd been my catalyst. I figured I owed him more than I could repay. Loyalty through his employment downturn seemed a good place to start. I couldn't help feeling angry with him at times, though what couples didn't fight?

Now Adrian had appeared as my life looked more dingy than I cared to admit. While he said all the right things and could kiss like a dream, was I considering Adrian as an easy substitute? After all, if I moved from Joel to Adrian, I wouldn't be alone again. Plus, having two sexy guys fighting over me sure was heady, even if I thought the occurrence more male hormones than my potency.

I didn't want to be a woman who bounced from man-to-man, looking for paradise in their eyes. Or their pants.

What was the path to becoming emotionally strong? How could I take charge? Stand behind my choices without second-guessing myself? Were strong women born or made?

My brain circled back to the Joel-Adrian dilemma. The choices I faced made me crazy.

I slid into bed and punched my pillow. A decision about this lifetime seemed further away than ever.

My dreams were filled with images of Joel and Adrian and myself from different eras, interacting either singly or in tandem. We all took turns as the villain or the hero. We'd played many scenes, hurt and loved each other many times.

I tossed and turned, waking with more questions than answers.

Chapter Nine

I blinked my eyes then took a deep breath while standing outside my building on Monday morning. Peeking from beneath my eyelids didn't change the scene or erase the bluish light. Or the low-pitched hum.

Damn it. I had to be at work in half an hour. This was no time for a woo-woo land visit.

A freaking horse and wagon stood at the curb. Correction. The non-existent curb. Joel sat on the wagon's bench. He had his boots up on the board before him; one elbow rested on the buggy's sideboard. Smoke curled from the cigar he held. The sunlight told me this image came from late afternoon rather than morning.

Huh. Somewhere along the line, I'd come to accept I truly did see different dimensions and/or timelines. I couldn't decide which. However, I kept the other lifetimes at an emotional distance, acknowledging everyone else's alternate identity but my own.

After last night, I knew I had to concentrate on learning the specific issues between Joel and myself. Then I could take action to heal our relationship or move on. Preferably both. And perhaps accept that Genevieve's life was my own.

I absorbed the picture, an overlay, with current times shaded like a watermark underneath. The overlapping scenes were confusing, so I concentrated on the past rather than the modern. Current day images receded as Chastity had promised. Yeah, baby, I was acing this Alice in Wonderland stuff.

This time the building behind me was a low wooden home with a small window beside the door. When Genevieve stepped off the porch, her full skirt swirled around her legs.

Her garment, a lavender and white striped dress, had a round lace collar and lace ribbons sewn down the arms. I'm not great with material types, but decided the gown was cotton or muslin. The waistline dropped into a vee-shape. Her feet were covered in worn tall lace-up boots that I suspected were her only good shoes. She wore white cotton gloves and a shawl, even though the day's heat had not dissipated. A small gathered bag lopped over her wrist. With her hair piled up, I thought she looked pretty darn good. I hoped for Genevieve's sake Sheriff Adam would agree.

"You gonna stand there and moon? Let's git a move on."

Once again, I watched myself as then Genevieve climbed onto the wagon and settled next to my then brother. They hadn't traveled long before he removed the cigar from his mouth and looked her over.

"Now listen here, Genevieve. I want you to stay away from that no-count sheriff tonight." He pointed his cigar at her. "No dancing. No talking. Don't even smile in his direction."

"I can't ignore the man, Jeb."

The scene wavered and lightened. The modern sound of automobiles bled through faintly. I balanced on my toes in frustration wanting to know more. Suddenly the old scene returned.

"How many times I gotta tell you? The bastard helped send our brother to prison," Joel/Jebediah said. "Some say he's hidin' Yankees up at his mountain cabin. Stay away from him." He flicked the reins over the horse's back and the historical scenario disappeared, fractured by modern traffic sounds.

My legs wobbled, and I moved to lean against my railing. Cars honked, school bus exhaust filled the air and sunshine warmed my face.

"I wonder what Chastity will say about this."

The answer sounded in my ear. "Chastity says I don't know what 'this' you mean."

I turned, grabbed my neighbor's upper arm, and squeezed. "You won't believe what happened." I looked her over. "Wait, what are you doing up and out before noon?"

She shrugged. "An appointment I couldn't put off." She strode toward my employer's building, pulling me along. "We can talk on the way. You don't want to be late today."

"Right." Howie itched to fire me and I didn't want to put Donna in the middle.

She entwined our arms. "So tell me what you're wondering I'll say?"

"I think I'm beginning to understand the multiple worlds stuff you talked about." As we walked, I told her about my short success in "tuning in" to the past.

"I'm *so proud* of you," Chastity said. "You're learning so quickly, and *just* in time. I wish I could help you more."

I stopped, my hand on her arm. "Wait a freaking minute. I get the feeling you know more than you're telling me."

Her mouth open and closed soundlessly. My eyes narrowed. "Uh huh. As I thought. You do know more, don't you?" I made a 'gimme' gesture. "Cough it up. I hate what's happening and you've got the answers to get me past this."

"N-n-no, I don't. I meant…I wanted to say—" She pulled me into a walk.

"Ah, ha."

"Really. I wish I *knew* more so I could *tell* you more. That's all I *meant*."

I searched her expression for answers, but none appeared. I was paranoid. If Chastity knew anything, she'd tell me. We were besties. Went with the territory.

"Never mind. I'm crazy with all this nutty stuff," I said. "I don't know why it can't be happening to you instead."

The familiar complaint rolled off my tongue without its normal heat. I'd gotten a glimpse of an alternate life and it drew my attention like a car accident on the interstate. I couldn't not look.

All my lives wouldn't be screwed up, would they? Maybe last night's dream of shifting places and changing faces had been caused by paint fumes.

I wished.

I slipped into my cubicle at three minutes before start time, shoving my bags under my desk and flipping on my computer in one practiced move. Howie popped up like a sprung Jack-in-the-Box two minutes later. He tapped his watch dial.

"Gabby, you should be ready to work at your start time, instead of waiting for your computer to boot up."

With his words, my monitor moved from black to the official J&J screensaver. I moved my mouse and checked the clock. "The company computer shows one minute to start time, Howie. Maybe the system is a little slow this morning. Should I call IT? See if anyone's reported a problem?"

I reached under my desk and flipped on my voice-activated recorder.

His full lips twisted. "No, never mind."

"Okay, then. Did you need something in particular?"

"Yes. Luckily, last Friday's report held correct numbers, but I had no opportunity to check the data prior to the meeting thanks to your late response."

No chance to backstab, you mean. You worm.

"I met the deadline you moved up by two hours with ten minutes to spare." My voice was level, thank goodness. I grasped my hands together on my lap. They wanted to wrap themselves around his neck but my brain didn't want me wearing orange.

"I don't mean disrespect Howie, but because you didn't send me the data until closing time Thursday, and then changed the deadline at the last minute, I was lucky to meet the goal. Under those circumstances, I'm glad the numbers were right." I congratulated myself on not pointing out he'd sat on the information I needed.

He pulled his looming dark storm cloud impression above me. "Gabby, you are my subordinate. If you wish to continue working here, you will meet my expectations."

His snide tone irked me. I worked to keep my temper, but the temptation to ream him out hovered. I remembered my higher goal and took a deep breath before answering.

"I'm sorry, I thought you said the report was

correct. As your *subordinate*, it's my job to provide you with impeccable data, right? Have I ever not done so?"

His baby blue eyes narrowed. "What are you saying? Exactly?"

"All my prior managers trusted me to do my job. I received stellar annual evaluations. My J&J history includes promotions and bonuses. I truly don't understand why you think I'd perform any differently for you."

"Your words sound like insubordination."

I shook my head and lowered my voice. "Howie, we don't need to be enemies. I'm not out to get you and I don't want your job. Why can't we get along?"

His stiff posture and gargoyle expression told me I'd said exactly the wrong thing, my reward for trying to prevent creating more bad karma/dharma in my life.

"Ms. Jung. Consider this a verbal warning. I will not tolerate your talking back. My request was clear. In future, all reports will be submitted at least thirty minutes in advance of deadline."

"Mr. Jackson. I respectfully request you provide report data with enough time to meet your new requirement."

His eyes narrowed to slits. "I will not tolerate much more of your lip. If I choose to provide data to you at 4:59 p.m., you'll have to work late, won't you." He smirked.

Donna cleared her throat loudly. I took several deep breaths before giving him a nod. "I understand."

"Consider yourself verbally warned, Gabby."

Donna snuck into my cubicle and reported Howie's progress to his office sotto voce. Meanwhile, I slammed my handbag and lunch into my desk drawers and pulled up my morning to-do list.

Donna hissed. "Gabriella. Why did you talk back to the toad? You know better."

"No sleep."

"Again? Is something wrong? Do you need to see a doctor? You're too young to have problems sleeping. Maybe you have sleep apnea. You should apply for a sleep study. Our insurance will cover."

My bad mood slipped away. "Nope. Bad dreams."

Donna tapped her finger against her lips. "Have you been taking melatonin? The stuff can cause bad dreams in some people. Better you should drink chamomile tea with a few drops of cat claw. Or valerian root."

"Cat claw?" I shuddered. "Cyrano would smother me in my sleep."

She shook her head. "It's a powdered root. Anyway, check with an herbalist."

"I'll ask my neighbor."

"Good." Her eyes looked worried. "A verbal warning isn't good, my friend. Howie is making his patented pre-termination moves."

"I know."

Howie begins hassling his targets on Fridays, probably to ruin their weekend with fear. After a while, he steps up his campaign to berating on Friday then threatening on Monday, with intermittent jabs during the workweek. He plays with people, sometimes ignoring them until they think he's fine with their performance before he swoops in for the kill.

"Is he around?"

Donna crouched below the cubicle's top edge and scanned the office. "Huddled in his office. He's holding up the newspaper's financial section but we know what that means."

We exchanged smirks. Howie's secretary had disclosed he used the financial section to mask his true reading material, an off-track racing form downloaded and printed through the company computer. When he "read" the main news, he had a men's magazine behind it. The ones featuring full-page foldouts. He thought no one knew. Ha. Even if he discovered his secretary had divulged his secret, he couldn't terminate her. She was his cousin, and a closer relation to the owners than he. Sometimes I enjoyed watching karma in action.

"You know, Donna, there's more than one way to clean his clock."

"What do you mean? Until he releases the data, you can't prepare the reports. With him super ticked off, he'll really screw with the numbers."

"Yeah, but there's gotta be a way around him. Before Howie instituted the change, I received direct data. He knows that I know he deliberately sits on the statistics. Changes them. I've got his number, and it pisses him off that I haven't let him screw me over."

"IT can't send you the numbers directly, not without Howie's permission."

I lowered my voice to a whisper. "Coyotes can be skinned if you have the right tools."

She held up her hand. "I don't want to know."

I hit her palm with mine in a default high five. "You won't."

After she left, I opened the spreadsheet I'd been keeping on interactions with Howie. Not only had I fully documented every conversation we held by date and time, I'd also noted those I'd overhead since he'd started his crusade to drive off every person with a brain. Although a clear picture of harassment had evolved, I knew I'd need more.

J&J has a large regional business, and other than Howie's department, the company doesn't have much turnover, good-paying jobs being scarce in Harteville. Thus, there was no dedicated human resources department other than a few clerks to shuffle papers. The VP handling employment issues is a Jackson. Enough said, right?

Figuring it'd be a case of his word against mine, I'd started orally recording our conversations. I pulled my voice-activated recorder from beneath my desk, edited out Donna and downloaded his latest "official warning" to a file titled "office birthdays and anniversaries." With any luck, Howie would be history sooner than later.

Then I contacted my long-time friend in IT. Her sister had been one of Howie's early victims. Her two best friends had run afoul of him not long after. As I said earlier, it's nice to see the bad guys get force-fed justice. In this case, the woman I needed help from had the auspicious name of Carma. I prayed she'd help me with my bitch.

Chapter Ten

Keeping busy at work should have helped me ignore Howie and from revisiting my strange dreams and weird visions. Instead, I spent way too much time wondering what would happen next. Once during the afternoon, I'd heard a low hum and run for the bathroom then deduced the sound came from a defective fan. The incident made me afraid I'd see the past when I least expected and get caught without a hiding place. By the time my shift ended, I'd become a basket case. Which is my excuse for responding as I did when Joel called not long after I arrived home.

"Hi, Gab, how're you doing?"

I didn't respond, unsure I wanted a conversation with him.

"Gab? I told you I'd call remember? Are you feeling okay?"

I sank into the closest chair. Cyrano jumped into my lap and butted my open hand. "Yes, I remember. Tough day, that's all."

"Oh, cool. I thought maybe you were still pissed at me." His voice dropped to a husky whisper. "I'd hate for that to happen."

Heat ran up my spine. Joel knew my buttons a little too well. "Actually, I'm still working through my mad. I just got home and I'm beat. Did you call to apologize? Or why exactly are we talking?"

"Geez, talk about crabby. I can call back later when you're over your bitch, um, when you feel better."

I shook my head. How did I get hooked into this mess? I forced a conciliatory note into my voice. "Well, the last time I saw you, you basically called me a slut, so pardon me, but I do wonder what's going on between us. Anything? Anything at all?"

His tone sounded like a mix between pissed off and mollifying. Huh. Like mine.

"Gab, look, I'm sorry for jumping to conclusions. I like what's mine staying mine, you know?"

A cold chill shook me from head to toe. "Are you saying I'm your possession?"

"No! No, I mean, ah, we've got a good thing going. I'd hate to lose you because some jerk horned in."

"Uh, huh." Fatigue swept me. All I wanted to do was run a bath, drink wine, and eat junk food, which would have been a good plan if I had any snacks or wine in the house.

"Look," his voice lowered into a deeper register. "I don't want trouble between us. I really am sorry I flew off the handle. I promise I'll treat you right."

I rubbed my temples to relieve the painful twinges. "Apology accepted. Now I really have to run."

"Where are you going?"

His interrogatory tone rang my warning bells. "I forgot to stop for food on the way home."

He breathed a sigh of what sounded like relief. "Let me take you out for dinner."

My eyebrows rose. "I thought you didn't have any money until your next check came?"

He cleared this throat. "Yeah, well, a buddy lent me a few bucks to tide me over."

I rubbed my temples. "Then you should hang on to your money. I'll nuke a frozen dinner."

"You want me to come over? Rub your feet? Or maybe a few other places?"

My skin itched, as if reminding me his last touches had irritated not soothed. "Thanks, but I'm pooped."

"Tomorrow?"

"My head is pounding, Joel, I can't think that far ahead."

"Oh, okay then. I'll phone after you've eaten, in case you change your mind. All right?"

"Fine."

We ended the call and I leaned back in my chair, watching as Cyrano jumped down and licked his shoulders. What the heck? Joel acted as sweet as he had when we'd first met. Before he began taking me and my wallet for granted. Maybe he'd gotten a job offer. No, he would have crowed the news all over town. I guessed he didn't like competition, though I'd given him little to worry about.

Although the kiss with Adrian almost qualified as cheating considering the thoughts and emotions his lips evoked. I must be crazy, thinking about giving Joel a chance simply because he'd promised to change. On the other hand, I knew I had to better understand our past. Good or bad, we had to play out our dealt hands.

My thoughts turned to Howie. Yet another man who used his charm to manipulate. The books Chastity had pushed on me explained the philosophy of a person's thoughts creating their environment. I must have had some shitty thoughts to end up where I was right now.

Crap. Chastity's "think good vibes" lecture could

mean more than I'd thought.

But Adrian was different. Wasn't he?

My dreams and the weird dimensional viewing stuff had helped me find the personal strength Chastity insisted I'd had all along. I also felt more comfortable with my intuitive feelings. The new inner knowledge helped me understand more about why I attracted men like Joel and Howie. I'd have to fix myself before I could accept Adrian.

Damn it. I had more lessons to learn and hated the idea.

My stomach didn't growl, it let out a roar. I hoped eating would ease my headache. I pulled myself from my chair, picked up my purse, and headed for the door. Damned if I didn't walk onto the sidewalk and into Adrian.

"Hey, Gabriella. Thought I'd stop by and see how you were doing."

"Why?"

"Why?" He rubbed his forehead with his fingertips. "Well because you zombie walked past me earlier. You didn't answer my calls, and I shouted your name more than once. I considered physically stopping you, but figured I'd better not. Are you okay?"

Sheesh. Everyone I talked with asked if I were okay. "Yes," I answered through clenched teeth. "I'm fine and dandy. Only I'd be even better if I could eat." I pointed to the corner. "I'm on my way to the store."

"Oh, right." He took a step back. "I have a sister. I know not to get in her way when she's craving chocolate every month."

It took my depleted brain cells a moment to interpret his comment. I closed my eyes. God, no, he didn't really mean his statement, did he? Was he really getting personal with a woman he barely knew?

"I mean, you know, I understand you might be feeling sensitive."

Yes, he really did mean what I thought. I opened my eyes and adhered a smile over what had to be red cheeks given the heat I felt on my face. "I'm only shopping for dinner." I moved to push past him then stopped. "Thanks for checking on me. I appreciate the thought."

His head tilted to the side. His slack jaw didn't lessen his cute factor, but simply made him more adorable.

""Really, you're sweet to care," I added.

His reply followed me as I walked off.

"Sweet? Shit. I just got the kiss of death."

****

"You said *what* to Adrian?" Chastity plopped her fist against her hip while Cyrano skittered from the room. "And you're trying to resolve things with Joel? Are you allowing misguided loyalty to sway your decisions?"

I straightened my spine. May as well start claiming my power, at whatever level, right now. "Joel lifted me up from a dark place and stuck with me. Well, until recently."

Her chin wobbled.

"I haven't forgotten that you helped too, Chastity. It's...I feel responsible. Would you like it if I walked away from you when you lost a job?"

Not that she'd understand having a job. My friend had a mysterious cash source that she'd never explained. I figured trust fund baby, but that didn't rationalize her living in my apartment building. My place wasn't a dump, but wouldn't someone with a ready cash supply choose a bigger life style? One more question without a clue to answering the mystery comprising Chastity.

"Joel is a *user*," she said. "He manipulates through charm and good looks. He weaseled into your life and you don't see his ambition."

"Oh, so I'm too dumb to know better?"

She gasped. "Gabriella, *no*." Her face paled. "That's *not* what I meant."

"Look, I know you've never liked Joel, but I have to come to terms with what he means or doesn't mean to me."

Her face regained some color. She nodded. "You're right. I'm wrong."

"It's not a matter of right or wrong. The situation *is*."

A smile twitched her lips. "You do know you sounded like me."

I sighed. "Yeah."

Her forehead wrinkled then smoothed. "Will you admit you need all the facts in order to make a decision?"

I could sense trouble in her question, but wasn't sure in which direction it laid. "Yeah, facts are good."

"Get your purse. We're going out. My treat for dinner."

"No, please no. I had a bad day at work. All I want is a bath and wine. Oh, look! I have one of the two right here at hand." I didn't mention my third wish was to open the junk food I'd just purchased.

She glanced at my half-full glass then caught my

gaze. "Take your bath. Then we're going out. There's something you need to see." She turned for the door then stopped and looked over her shoulder. "No excuses."

I nuked and wolfed an appetizer to take the edge off my hunger then fed Cyrano while the bath water ran. A search for reading material began, and not one of Chastity's book picks. A bad feeling I'd hear more on those topics later tonight swirled in my thoughts.

Retrieving the thin romance novel I'd buried in my nightstand drawer after I'd met Joel, I checked the blurb to ensure I hadn't already read this one. The hero on the cover looked a bit too much like Adrian for comfort.

Steam tendrils rose from the scented water. Shedding my clothes in record time, I eased into the water. Before I could open my romantic escape on paper, I heard a low hum.

No, damn it, no.

Followed by a blue glow filling the bathroom. *Shit.*

The vision faded in slowly, like watching an art film effect. I stood in a large hall. The room was lit with lanterns, casting shadows on the space's edges. A small stage held musicians playing violins, banjo and guitar. Dancers filled the floor following the dance caller's steps. Several tables were set up, holding dessert selections and what appeared to be punch.

Many attendees were dancing, but a small number of men huddled together in one dark corner, passing what looked like a small stone jug. Older women shot them dirty looks from across the room, but the drinkers, who included Jebediah, were clueless.

My toe tapped my bathtub's side as I watched the dancers. Not enough bass, and I'm not a big blue-grass fan, but lively. The dancers were red-faced and laughing. Even as an observer, I could sense joy in the air. Given these gatherings were probably few and far between, the evident pleasure on everyone's face was understandable.

Sheriff Adam was making his way toward Genevieve until an older woman stopped him. Based on her posture, appearance and stern expression, I intuited she was either the schoolteacher or a preacher's wife. I watched as Genevieve checked Jebediah's location then looked back to Adam. The older woman with Adam pointed toward the huddled men and he stared in their direction. He patted the woman's hand obviously reassuring her, but his attention remained across the room.

I watched as he paused, switching his attention between the men and Genevieve. The huddle broke up, the men scattered. His frown smoothed. He turned on his heel, headed in her direction.

"May I have this next dance, Miss Genevieve?"

She gulped. "Why, yes, Sheriff. I'd be pleased."

He took her hand in his larger one. Genevieve relaxed and lost herself in his gaze, her attention solely focused on Adam. He twirled her into the eddy of music and dancers.

Then the music screeched to a halt, and she was pulled from Adam's embrace. Her brother loomed. Priscilla, the town's richest man's daughter and a nasty gossip—I knew all this somehow—stood at his shoulder, her hair mussed. Her frown was a feminine match to the glower Jebediah wore.

"I should have known you'd dance with that no-count against my express wishes." He wrapped his large paw around Genevieve's upper arm. "This dance ends now."

This lifetime observation stuff was limited to sight and sound for the most part. Yet, I didn't need a sense of smell to know Jeb had taken a few too many swigs from the jug based on his swaying and blood-shot eyes.

Adam smoothly peeled Jebediah's hand from Genevieve's arm. "You can't hold on to her forever," he said. "Genevieve deserves her own home and children."

Jebediah snorted. "With you, I suppose. No sirree. Not if I have a say."

"I know you'd like her to cook and clean for you until you die, but that jest ain't right," Adam said. "Your pa would have let her go. Find yourself a wife, Jebediah. I'm sure Miss Priscilla would oblige you. No good will come of keeping Genevieve locked away on your farm."

"Keep your opinions to yourself. My sis ain't gonna be keepin' company with no traitor. Especially no Yank sympathizer who arrested our brother."

A gasp ran around the room.

"Jeb, it's not Adam's fault Micah fell in with the wrong crowd," Genevieve said. "You know our brother wouldn't listen to anyone but Pa. And with Pa lying in the graveyard this past year and more, wasn't gonna take much before Micah came to standing before a judge."

"The *sheriff* ain't to be trusted. What about them strangers seen around his cabin?"

Something told me Adam had been ambushed with the truth. I had a feeling Jebediah was right about the sheriff and his isolated mountain cabin. I'd seen enough of Genevieve's life to intuit hers was a Confederate household, but I also knew from my recent reading that many settlers in the North Carolina mountains didn't hold with slavery or being told which side to support. If Adam was hiding Yanks or spying, he and Genevieve were on opposite sides in the War of Northern Aggression.

Adam didn't respond to the taunts, but his jaw tightened. I watched, afraid Jebediah and his hothead friends fueled by cheap whiskey would do something stupid.

The older woman I'd seen speaking with Adam bustled forward. He put a restraining hand on her arm. "You don't want a part of this, Mrs. Maddox."

"Hush, Adam. Jebediah, you've had too much to drink." She held up her palm when he opened his mouth to speak. "No, don't you speak, young man. Your words have caused enough trouble tonight. Why, the Sheriff is no more a Yankee traitor than I am."

Lantern light highlighted Mrs. Maddox's blond hair. Her hand gesture and blue eyes struck a chord of recognition. Chastity. Playing teacher again.

She continued her harangue. "Shame on you. It's time you apologized to both Adam and your sister. They were doing nothing more than enjoying a dance." She sniffed. "Something you should do more instead of gulping down the rot gut your friend Bobby Vance brews behind his pig sty. You'll all go blind one of these days."

Yep. Pure Chastity.

Jebediah's face turned red. He pulled his arm from Adam's grasp and pointed a shaking finger at Genevieve. "I'll be waiting outside. It's time we left."

He stumbled across the now quiet dance floor and out.

The scene faded and I examined my now wrinkled fingers. The novel I'd meant to read had fallen next to the tub, the Adrian-like model's face hidden in the rug.

I climbed from the lukewarm water and dried off. The parallel of my alternate life to this one was clear. No wonder I had found totally trusting Adrian problematic. We'd not only been on opposite sides in the national conflict, he'd sent another then brother to prison. The lifetime or alternate dimension I kept seeing had to be the pivotal one Madame L. had mentioned. Knowing how to incorporate that knowledge stumped me.

A few moments later, I knocked on Chastity's door. Normally I'd have walked in as freely as she did to my apartment, but since Mike had entered the scene, I'd decided on circumspection.

She threw open the door and pulled me inside. "What the heck happened? The energy pulsed so hard, I could almost see it through the walls."

That said something, given my bathroom is on the furthest wall from her living room.

Describing visions felt like old hat, they'd occurred so regularly in the past few days.

"Water is a conduit for spiritual energy," she said.

"Okay, so I won't take baths for the foreseeable future. Showers, either."

"Silly. I'll show you how to protect your energetic field."

Pondering her words, I wondered about her statement. Nothing I'd seen or felt had been negative. Did she know something she wasn't telling me? I voiced my questions.

"No, I want you to feel comfortable with the process."

"What process?"

"Observing and healing your past through dimension hopping."

"Right." If nothing else, I knew my weird experiences would help me decide how to live the only life I could reliably dial in on every day.

"You know," she said, "I've come to realize you're right about Joel. Coming to terms with your life and its permutations is your mission. I've got only one thing to say."

I braced myself.

She grasped my shoulders and caught my eye. "Demand the respect you deserve." Chastity dropped her hands. "Now let's go to dinner. There's something you need to see." She tilted her head. "You can't go looking like *that*."

"Huh?" I scanned my clothes. "No spots, stains, rips or tears. I should be good to go."

"You need to look your best."

Her tone scared me. What did she want to show me?

As she hustled me back into my apartment, my phone rang.

"Hey, Gab," Joel said. "Listen, something's come up, so I won't be checking in later. Hope you don't mind, but I'm meeting with a guy who might have a job lead. I want to jump on it. You know how hard I've been looking."

"Great news, Joel. I hope the lead pans out for you." I didn't dare look at Chastity. I could sense her smirk from across the room.

In a surprising move, she ignored the call and picked up our earlier conversation. "As I said, you need to look your best. I like the gold silk blouse with the leaf pattern you've paired with tailored black slacks. Classy. But something is missing." She rested her chin on her palm. "You need more make-up."

"I already put on blush and eyeliner. And I have lipstick right here." I reached in my pocket and pulled out a tube I'd originally purchased in high school.

She stepped back and leveled a finger at my lip color. "Toss the tube in the trash right now. It's probably infested with viruses without a known cure."

"Doubt it. I haven't used it often enough to attract bugs."

She grabbed the tube from my hand. "You will not be applying this. Not again." To punctuate her statement, she threw my uncapped lipstick into the trash, directly atop discarded ravioli. The tube sank into the tomato sauce. Yew.

"Come." She pulled my arm. "We may have enough time to take care of business."

Fifteen minutes later, my face sported more make-up than I'd used in my entire life. She surveyed me with her jaw resting on her palm. "You're ready. Let's go."

My heart pounded. What would I see tonight? And why did the prospect scare me shitless?

Chapter Eleven

A surprise awaited in the hall outside my apartment. Adrian, garbed all in black, looked yummier than a box of my favorite dark chocolate truffles.

He grabbed my arm and steadied my astonished teetering. His pupils darkened. His throat moved in a swallow.

"You sure clean up well." A wince flashed across his face followed by a small grin. "I'm sorry the paint from yesterday washed out of your hair. You looked good with pale green highlights."

"I thought I'd try out a new look."

He scanned me from head to foot and back. "I approve."

My face heated. I turned and locked my door. "Chastity and I were on our way to dinner."

"I know," he said. "Mike and I are joining you."

Great. Chasity's work again. She'd said she understood I needed to work things out with Joel but then she planned a double date. I didn't understand her chess move, so I punted, to mix game metaphors.

Mike drove us to a restaurant I'd heard about but never expected to patronize. Zoe's, an upscale bistro specializing in organic, locally sourced, and seasonal food prepared by an inventive European-trained chef, had a zealous patronage. As you can imagine, the prices did not compare to your local fast food emporium.

Reservations were almost impossible. I wondered who knew whom to get us in at the last minute.

Chastity half-turned and looked at me from the front seat. "Do not start. This is my treat. Don't even think about quid pro quo."

I opened my mouth but wasn't given an opportunity to speak. Adrian had already slid from the car and held his hand out to help me exit. Because Mike and Chastity's long legs carried them to the restaurant faster than I could move, I was out-maneuvered once again.

Inside, I saw a sign announcing a jazz combo would be playing later to honor Zoe's third anniversary. As we were seated, I noticed a drum set, amplifiers, and a small dance floor had been set up at one end of the room.

Zoe's was everything I'd imagined, starting with the reclaimed wooden floors. One long wall to our left, painted in deep coral, was covered with art created from recycled metal and hammered copper. A burnished wood bar obviously carved in the late 1800s took up the wall to our right. Customers seated at tables best described as an eclectic mix filled the space in between. Although food scents hovered over the room, nothing hit my nose as overpowering. Fresh flowers, linen tablecloths, and candlelight completed the scene.

I whispered to Chastity, "Did you say you wanted to show me something only to get me here with Adrian? I thought you wouldn't interfere."

She shook her head. "I'm not butting in, only providing you an opportunity to have all the facts in hand. Wait. You'll see."

A chill ran up my spine, unsure I wanted to see

what she hinted at.

After a dinner so good I'd be dreaming about it for years, the combo began playing an up tempo song.

Adrian grasped my hand. "We shouldn't waste this great music. Care to dance?"

"Sure."

Damn, the man could shake it. I tried keeping my eyes off his swiveling hips, but no woman with half a brain would have missed watching his moves. I mean to say. Phew.

When the faster music segued into a slow dance, Adrian pulled me into his arms and swung me into a breathtaking turn. His combined spicy cologne, hard muscles, and heat may have caused my failed lung capacity. I wasn't in the mood to quibble. We moved as if we'd danced together for years.

As I closed my eyes and my brain lost the "don't snuggle with Adrian fight," I caught a frightening glimpse. My muscles tightened into one rigid mass. The man walking onto the dance floor looked like Joel. Wait, he didn't look like Joel, he *was* Joel. Holding a woman in a red dress so close, I thought they'd been welded together.

Adrian leaned back to catch my eye. "What's wrong?" With his back to the other couple, he hadn't noticed my erstwhile boyfriend.

"Nothing." I ducked my head to hide my suddenly damp eyes. "Someone I thought I knew."

He held me like I'd suddenly become fragile porcelain. Maybe I had. By the time the song ended, I'd pulled myself together enough to flash him a smile. He tucked my arm over his and led us back to the table.

Chastity and Mike were already seated. She

glanced at me, and her forehead wrinkled. Before I could tell her about Joel, amplifier feedback squealed and the restaurant lights flashed. Her glance sharpened. She said something I couldn't hear to Mike, grabbed my hand, and headed for the ladies.

Before I got my feet under me properly, I heard the low hum and saw the particular blue flashes preceding a blast to the past. Damn it all. Time traveling while standing in the ladies room line didn't top my smart ideas list.

My friend steered us into the alley.

"I'm here, Gabriella. I won't leave and no one will get close."

Those were the last twenty-first century words I heard.

Square dance music and chatter filled the air as I stood outside a large wooden barn. Jebediah and Genevieve stood toe to toe before me.

"Jeb are you or are you not going to marry Priscilla?"

"None of your business, Sis."

I watched my alternative self gather herself. I anticipated her next words though her brother didn't. "I deserve to know. Pa left the farm to you, but he told me it'd be my home, too. I was there when he asked for your promise to see me settled."

He adjusted his hat. "I'll see you settled, to anyone but the sheriff. My buddy Deke will have you. Don't know why he'd take you on. You can't cook worth a damn."

"I want no part of Deke. He's a drunk, a gambler, and he mistreats his horse."

Jebediah laughed. "What's making you so high and

mighty all of a sudden? Listening to old biddy Maddox again?" He put his hands on his hips. "You'll marry who I say."

Genevieve grasped his arm. "You know there's bad blood between Priscilla and me. If you're gonna marry her, I want to know."

"You think Pa would want to see you making up to a Yank?"

"The only reason Pa chose the South is because he believed the Constitution allowed for legal secession. He'd no more have a slave working the land than most others in town would."

"North Carolina is a Confederate state. Them what don't like it can cross the Mason-Dixon."

Genevieve's hands shook so hard her purse jerked in her hands.

Adam suddenly stood behind Genevieve. "Everything all right out here? Folks could hear you shouting, Jebediah." He leaned closer to Genevieve. "Couldn't hear the words, though."

Jebediah sneered. "This is a family affair, Sheriff."

"Miss Genevieve? You're shaking. I do believe you'd be better off inside." Adam offered his arm. "May I escort you?"

"You may be a lawman but you got no right to touch my sister without permission."

"You're right." Adam caught her eye. "Would you like to go in, Miss Genevieve?

She nodded. "Yes, thank you." She took his arm and they turned toward the door.

"We ain't finished, sheriff."

Genevieve stopped and turned. "Jeb, you are a disgrace. It's time you took responsibility for the farm and started your own family. I'll be leaving as soon as I can pack."

He snorted. "Right. Like you have a place to go."

She threw back her shoulders. "I do, as a matter of fact."

His eyes narrowed. "No, you don't. Your place is with me. On the farm."

She shook her head. "No, Jeb. Not anymore. Make an honest woman out of Priscilla. With a little work, you two can make a good life together." Her eyes filled with tears. "You'll always be my brother, but I can't countenance your behavior any longer."

I blinked my eyes and the scene dissipated. Chastity held my hands. The brick wall behind my back held the day's heat. I shook with emotion.

Luckily my friend didn't ask me questions, but simply said, "You're back."

I nodded. "Genevieve is moving from the farm."

Gathering my scattered thoughts and tattered feelings, I forced a smile. "Let's go back in. I think I need the bathroom."

What I really needed was prodigious amounts of wine and those pills that wipe memory. You know, the ones in the Jim Carrey movie about eternal sunshine.

"I apologize, Gabriella."

"Why?"

"I didn't expect you seeing Joel with another woman would trigger an episode."

"Ah, you saw her, huh?" I shrugged. "I wanted more information and you helped me obtain it. Not your fault he's a liar."

Anger flooded my blood stream. "Ass wipe." My hands fisted. "I should go back in there and tell him off right now." My voice mimicked his. "I'm meeting with a guy who might have a lead on a job. I want to jump right on it." I snorted. "Right. Pretty obvious what he's jumping."

My initial anger was supplanted with hurt. How could Joel do this? Why couldn't he be honest and break it off? Why did he sneak around? Worse, he apparently thought I wouldn't find out about Miss Red Dress. Or maybe he didn't care if I did.

Do you know anyone who likes to get duped? Me neither. I bounced between anger, hurt, and self-disgust faster than a lottery ball whizzed around in the clear-sided barrel used for drawings. I wanted to march back inside and plant myself before Joel but wasn't sure the embarrassment would be worth the public confrontation. Did I really want Adrian to see my meltdown?

Chastity didn't speak but she tightened her grip on my hand.

"Don't worry. I won't cause a scene."

""You've got it wrong, sweetie," she said. "I can sense what you want and I'll hold your handbag for you. Unless you need it as a bludgeon. First though, take some deep breaths."

Curiously, the inhalations worked magic, and my wish to create an angry scene dissipated. The hurt hadn't left, nor had I reconciled myself to having Joel's lies thrown in my face. Even though Chastity had led me here tonight, probably knowing what I'd see, I'd needed the wake-up call. Damn. I wished I could scrub my eyeballs clean and wipe out memory cells, too. Unfortunately, life doesn't work that way.

We rejoined Adrian and Mike, but my mood had

been destroyed.

Joel and the woman in red had gone. My innocence and loyalty had taken a huge hit. I had serious thinking ahead. The kind I couldn't put off any longer.

****

Adrian flicked my nipples with a two-inch paintbrush. My body lifted from the bed and slammed against his hard muscles. Damn. There was no give, just solid strength against my length. I purred.

He threw the brush aside, running his hands over my breasts while his mouth moved to warm my abdomen with kisses and hot breath. Not only were his muscles—all of them—hard as Grandfather Mountain, he knew how to kiss. And how. And where. Yeah, baby.

His mouth continued its pre-winter journey south and my hormones continued to rage. He'd find a hundred year flood when he finally reached my inner thighs. Holy Incipient Climax. I wanted Adrian. All of him. Now.

A large weight landed on my chest. "Oof. What the hell?"

I opened my eyes. Cyrano stood on my chest. "No, sweetie, not now. Adrian is going to…disappear?"

My gaze scanned the room. I was alone but for my cat with bad timing. Though my body hummed with sexual passion, unfulfilled consummation had the starring role. I extended my arms over my head while Cyrano performing his own morning stretch.

"Couldn't have been a dream, Cyrano. Dang. That felt real." Right down to the sexual juices moistening my vagina.

I checked my clock. "Not only am I not dreaming, it's time to get up for work. Crap."

I swung my feet onto the floor and stepped on something not there when I fell asleep.

I lifted my foot and took a closer look. "Holy Paint Fumes." Blood rushed to my head. Yep, a two-inch paintbrush had appeared in my bedroom.

I'm not sure how I completed my morning ritual other than figuring I stumbled through my normal preparations by rote.

At least I didn't face Monday morning. Even Howie couldn't make this "I've been cheated" feeling any worse.

****

"Howie's pitching a fit," Donna muttered as she walked past my desk.

"What's new?" I offered her my candy dish filled with miniature chocolate bars. She grabbed one and tore into it like an angry badger.

"He thinks someone here is out to get him."

I leaned back in my chair. "Golly, for once he's right. Should I mark this day on my calendar?"

She snorted then looked over her shoulder. "He's been in and out of his office all morning. Something's got his tail twisted."

"Really? He assigned me more projects this morning. I haven't lifted my head since I arrived."

"Keep your head down, then." She tossed the candy wrapper in my trash and left.

My phone rang. Before I could answer, I heard Howie's dulcet tones. "Gabby, get in here. Now."

As he was already hanging up, I didn't bother answering. Yes, he's Mr. Charm.

He couldn't expect me to have his report complete already? Sure he would, but I had a feeling something else hung in the malevolent smog making up his office atmosphere.

I brushed off my lap and checked to ensure all my blouse buttons were fastened. Then I ran a moist towelette over my shoes, in case they were dirty. My fingernails received a quick buff then I smoothed my eyebrows. I grabbed my recorder, turned it on and stuffed it inside a manila file folder. Ready, I stood and headed toward Howie's office at a leisurely pace.

Did Howie know I stalled? Sure. Did I care? After the emotional trifecta of seeing Joel with Red Dress Woman, waking with my girl parts humming and left waiting, and getting another rush job dumped in my lap, my bullshit quotient had been filled for the week. I wouldn't lay odds on keeping my job. Especially a job I wasn't sure I could stomach any longer.

"You wanted to see me, Howie?"

He reclined in his chair but didn't invite me to sit. "Yes. Have you finished the report I assigned you?"

I held back a sigh. "Do you mean the one you gave me two hours ago, the one you assigned yesterday, or one of the two dozen I've taken on in the past six months?"

His pupils contracted to small dots. "Your tone sounds suspiciously like insubordination."

Now I let my sigh free. "Howie, I can't answer your question unless you specify. Which report do you mean?"

He tapped his forefinger on the desk. "This morning's report. It was a simple request. You should be done by now."

Not sure whether my recorder would pick up his voice from a distance, I moved closer. "Well, I've had trouble putting together the numbers."

"I'm not surprised. I noticed your friends stopping by to visit on a regular timetable."

I jumped in with the facts before my temper exploded. "The difficulty is with the numbers, Howie. I'm afraid the data is incomplete."

"I gave you everything I had."

"The report can't be completed without all the statistics. You've asked for a year-to-date overview, but the accounts receivable numbers are from two weeks ago. Payables data is from three weeks ago. Even with an adjusted report date, the numbers would be wrong." I took a deep breath. "No one could assemble a correct report using your data."

"Are you saying I don't know my job?"

"Not at all, but I thought you'd want to provide correct reports. After all, the statistics coming from me reflect directly on your reputation."

Now two fingers tapped on his desk in a staccato rhythm. "You will use the numbers I provided. The report is due in," he checked his watch, "thirty minutes." He clenched his fingers into a fist. "No excuses. Your work has dropped in both quantity and quality. If the report isn't on my desk on time, you'll move from oral to written warnings. Clear?"

Not trusting myself, I nodded. Then, remembering I needed a recorded answer, I said, "Yes."

He made a shooing motion. "Then get to it."

I walked to the bathroom and, after checking I was alone, played back a portion of our conversation. My trusty recorder had captured everything I needed. I hustled back to my desk, completed my ongoing spreadsheet then churned out the report Howie wanted.

He probably figured it'd be his word against mine in a termination hearing, but I'd had it with his ass-wipe ways. Maybe the spreadsheet and recordings wouldn't mean much in the long run, but they sure made me feel better about my life in the trenches. Putting up with lying scum buckets wasn't in my job description.

Chapter Twelve

"I don't believe this crap day." I slammed my coffee mug down and pushed it aside.

"Ah, ah, watch your words," Chastity said.

"Okay," I groused. You tell me if it's crap." I ignored her glare and continued. "There I was, about to get it on with Adrian when the dream ended." I crossed my arms and huffed. "What's with that?"

Chastity yawned. "You're not ready."

"Tell that to my ovaries."

My friend squinted and replayed her yawn. "Some part of you is unresolved."

"Inform my quivering lips."

She drank her tea then pursed her lips. "I'm serious. You saw Joel with someone else and the same night you have an erotic dream about Adrian. Coincidence?" She tapped her fingernails on the table. "Don't think so. Not now, not anywhere else."

I sat back and considered Chastity's words. She was right. I hadn't officially sent Joel packing. A portion of my emotions remained tied up with him. Dang. My stomach muscles clenched and based on her reaction, my realization was clearly written on my face.

"See? You have to cut your misbegotten link to Joel, first." She paused and a smile lit her face and the room. "Can I be here when you tell him? Huh? Please?"

After I choked back a laugh, I shook my head. "No.

For the first time in months, maybe years, I feel strong. I can do this."

She rubbed her hands together and cackled in a poor imitation of the Wicked Witch of the West. "I've been waiting for this to happen as long as the jerk's been coming around." She tapped her teeth with her fingernail. "Remember I'm right next door."

Putting on my best fake Southern accent I said, "Bless your heart. Thank you for your support." I inhaled through my nose. "Really, I appreciate you. Even knowing he's a cheater, I still feel bad for some reason."

"Stop blaming yourself. You did nothing wrong except trusting a creep."

Something I'd done before and lived through. I could handle the phone call with class.

Taking advantage of my resolute attitude, I dialed Joel. I meant to tell him off over the phone, but on hearing his voice, I realized I needed to see his face when I dumped him. Perhaps my experience as the dumpee had made me soft, though I preferred to think I was strong enough to handle the break maturely. For whatever reason, I asked him to stop by.

Not long after, I heard Joel's distinctive double knock. "Come in." I'd left the door open so I wouldn't be in his proximity.

"So why am I here, Gab?" He looked at his watch. "Can you make it quick? I've got an appointment in a few minutes."

"Oh, a follow-up to your interview? How did your meeting go, by the way? Did you get a jump on the job? I think those were your words?"

He scratched his head. "Oh, yeah. The interview. I

think I've got a real chance."

I debated about painting him into a corner, but couldn't stand his smarmy act one moment more. I threw my shoulders back and lifted my chin. "I think we should stop dating."

"What? Why, because I haven't been dancing attention on you for the past several days? Geez, I needed a break. You haven't been Miss Personality. We barely go out as it is."

"I haven't wanted to go out because I pay for us both. It's not like you ever offered to take me to a place like Zoe's."

"What?" His face turned magenta. "Zoe's is out of your league." His voice softened. "I mean it's expensive. I told you I'd make it all up once I had a job."

"True." I nodded. "But I saw you. Last night. At Zoe's. With a woman welded to your side on the dance floor. Red dress? Dark hair?"

"I had to be nice to her. She's my job contact."

"Right. Then why do I think you're lying?"

His expression hardened. "Me, lying? Ungrateful bitch. After all I've done for you."

"All you've done?" I hiccupped. I held up my hand palm out. I gulped air. "Okay, sure, dinners out—my expense. Dinners in—my expense." I raised my index finger. "And don't forget lunches and breakfast. The loan to cover your rent and car payments. Guess I was paying for the few times you got it together to pity fuck me."

Shit. I closed my eyes. The comment had come from nowhere conscious, but once said, colored the air like a sulfurous emission.

"You're not bad in the sack. Not the best I've ever had." He shrugged. "Better than some."

How do you insult me? Let me count the ways. What had I ever seen in this guy? Oh, right. He'd acted like he wanted me and that's all I'd needed. I mentally shook my head. Chastity had been so right. I owed my friend big time for years into the foreseeable future. Who knew what my debt was from other worlds and times? I shivered.

He raised his hand in a *Godfather* gesture. "I know what this is really about. Some idiot shows you a little attention and you're all over him. He's a player."

My breath escaped in a huff. Wasn't there a saying about seeing your own truth reflected in others? No wonder Joel interpreted Adrian's actions as a ploy. "You should know."

His hand dropped. "What?" His low voiced question seemed more a threat and sent chills racing down my arms.

"I'm saying you've used me for the last time." The pressure on my chest lifted, my thoughts cleared.

His face darkened. "What do you mean?"

"This isn't working. I can't do this anymore."

"Fine, Gab. I'll leave. Don't think you can come crawlin' later. Know what I mean? Not my problem when geek man dumps you."

He looked me up and down. My skin crawled.

"Don't know why I bothered spending time with you in the first place." His face morphed into a sneer. "You're nothing but an Ice Queen." He strutted out.

I took a huge breath and collapsed onto the couch.

My teeth nibbled my lower lip. Could Joel be right? Maybe the only action I'd get with Adrian was in my dreams. I shook my head. Didn't matter. A dream lover was better than one who abused my trust and loyalty. I had a fresh start.

Moments after the door slammed shut behind my former boyfriend, Chastity knocked at the door and peeked in. "You okay?"

I nodded. "Yeah, you know, I actually feel pretty good."

"Oh?"

"Yep. For the first time, I've stood up for myself with a man who thought my only purpose was a place for him to wipe his feet. Gotta say, I'm proud of myself." Even if scared shitless of what my life would become.

"Phew." She dropped onto the chair. "I worried you might back down."

"Moi?" I shook my head. "Joel told me not to come crawling when Adrian dumped me." I caught her eye. "You know what? I may not have a future with Adrian, but I won't ever crawl to Joel. I'm feeling I can live with myself as I am." Chill bumps raised on my arms with those words.

"You took a huge step." She leaned forward. "Besides, remember what Madame LaMere said about your true love's name having A and C initials. Although, even without her prediction, anyone can see the sparks flying when you and Adrian are together."

I shrugged. "I think jumping from man to man is silly."

"You're not bed hopping, you're finally moving into position to realize your life's mission. Letting Joel go was the first step."

"Life's mission? You had to raise that topic, didn't

you."

"Look, Gabriella, your Genevieve timeline had a similar event with her leaving the farm. Even though cosmic time is fluid, filled with potential, these two changes are following the same track. Separation is only an illusion remember? Your possible, probable, alternate, and parallel lives are united. It's time for you to determine what you want."

I struggled with her words. "You mean I should declare my desires, right?"

"Yes, that and more. You've lived according to everyone else's wishes for you rather than your truth. Don't you want to make your dreams a reality?"

"Shoot." I blew a long breath. "I get it and you're right. I've been settling and compromising my entire life."

She stood. "Take some time and think about what you want, what stirs your passions."

"Thanks for hanging in with me," I said. "I appreciate you."

"I know, Gabriella. Even when you act snotty, I feel the love."

"Go on, get gone or I'll think we're having a Kodak moment and grab my camera."

She pulled me into a tight hug. "Have I mentioned how proud I am of you?"

Her hug reassured me I wasn't alone. I had a loving friend; silk kimono, detox tea, weird books, and all. How could I go wrong? "Life is but a dream, sha-boom, sha-boom."

She shook her head and left. Although she hadn't raised the topic, I knew my real work lay in wait.

I poured a glass of wine, raising it in a salute to

myself before taking a swallow. The similarity between my life and Genevieve's was too clear to miss. Or rather between my lives in two different times, names, and appearances.

But one thing had been bugging me. What happened after the scene I watched faded out? Did time pass at the same speed in all lives? So if it's Tuesday night here, is it Tuesday for Genevieve? And where did she go when I stopped viewing?

One day soon I'd have to get comfortable with the idea that I was Genevieve. Those fractured images of her life weren't a movie.

I looked about the room, hoping I'd see a certain blue glow, but nothing changed.

Thinking about Genevieve's dilemma raised the image of Sheriff Adam. I couldn't quite release the feeling I shouldn't totally trust the man. He had a dark edge, possibly the product of the times. Living over a century earlier, even in a relatively settled section of North Carolina, wasn't the OK Corral. But a lawman dealt with society's dregs, no matter the time.

Had the sheriff been a Yankee spy? Could my former life memories have crossed the parallel and caused my discomfort? Had Adam misused Genevieve, or rather, the me living then? Or was I so afraid of trusting myself, I didn't want to put my faith in anyone? I didn't know, and fear I wouldn't like the answers crept into my heart.

Deciding to set my concerns aside, I pulled out a pad and pen. I'd begin by listing the things I wanted in my world. Couldn't hurt.

****

I sat at my desk the following afternoon, wishing

Howie would forget about my existence for the rest of the day. Hope springs eternal, right?

Turning to my monitor, I saw a quick flash of light. Then came a sudden, severe bout of vertigo. The screen before me flickered then a scene from the past appeared in full. Cripes. Now what? A *Little House* rerun?

Adam stood at a screen door, his hat in his hands. He nodded. "Miss Genevieve."

"Sheriff Adam."

My alternate self opened the door wide. Accepting the non-verbal invitation, he ducked inside.

"Are you settling in here with Mrs. Maddox? Can I do anything to help?"

"Thanks, but I'm doing fine, Sheriff. Mrs. Maddox is a treasure. I'm quite happy here."

"Good." He shuffled his feet. "I wondered if perhaps you'd like to accompany me for dinner one evening?"

"I'd like that, Sheriff."

He shifted his hat from hand to hand. "Adam. I'd enjoy hearing you use my name without the title."

She ducked her head. "Yes, Adam."

"Would Wednesday night suit you? I'll come by about five o'clock."

"I'd like that. Adam."

He nodded and stepped to the door. "I look forward to Wednesday dinner."

Genevieve blushed. "Me too."

Mrs. Maddox bustled up as Genevieve watched Adam disappear around a corner. "My, our sheriff certainly is a handsome man, don't you agree? Did I hear correctly? Now I wasn't eavesdropping, I happened to walk down the hall as you were speaking.

You did agree to have dinner with Adam, didn't you?"

Genevieve's mouth dropped open, but she remained silent.

"Wouldn't surprise me one bit if he starts walking out with you now you're in town," Mrs. Maddox said. She rubbed her hands together. "Won't that set the cats among the pigeons?"

Genevieve's hand fluttered over her dress's neckline. "It's dinner. He knows I could use a friend, is all."

Mrs. Maddox leveled a look at her. "Hmph. Friends my eye." She wiped her hands on her apron. "Listen to me, Genevieve. Adam's one good-looking man. He'll provide for his woman. Treat her like gold. Plenty of females in this town would give their back teeth for a night out with Adam. I know. I've seen them lined up to bring him dinner." She shook her head. "The man must have a cast iron stomach."

She shook her finger. "Now listen, missy. A chance like this comes along once in a lifetime." She cocked her head to the side. "And to make sure you enjoy yourself, you need a new dress. We'll head for the general store right after I take my pies from the oven."

"But Mrs. Maddox, I don't have money for a new dress. And I'm the one should be making the pies in exchange for your kindness."

The older woman waved her hand like she shooed flies. "Told you not to worry. You can pay me back after you get on your feet." Her head tilted. "Not that you'll need to find work, not given what I suspect is on Adam's mind. I only wish he—"

"He, what?"

"Never mind. Maybe this God-forsaken war will

end before any more of the men in town join up. Fathers fighting against their sons. Brothers on opposite sides. Whoever thought our country would come to this?"

The scene faded from my computer monitor, but the sick feeling caused by Mrs. Maddox's last words remained. Now I had a clue to the uneasiness I felt about Adrian's sincerity. To a Southern girl during the Civil War, Adrian posed a threat on more than one front. If he were a Yankee sympathizer, she'd be challenged philosophically. If he went to war and didn't return, she'd be ravaged emotionally.

I had a feeling, a certainty the key to learning the truth about Adrian's dark edge, why I didn't totally trust him, would be found sooner than later, unless the hallucinations stopped first.

Problem was, I didn't know if I wanted the knowledge.

"What's so exciting about a blank screen, Gabby?"

I looked up and blinked, unsure whether Howie scowling at me from my cubicle entrance was a hallucination. The mountain never went to Mohammad, if you catch my drift.

Mount Howie held out his hand and snapped his fingers. "The Coleman report. Now."

His face morphed, taking on a feminine cast. Holy Shades of Priscilla. Another piece of the past fell into place. Priscilla had abused Genevieve, and Howie did the same.

I pulled the Coleman report folder from my desk drawer, shoved it in his hands and stumbled from my cubicle.

"Where do you think you're going? Get back here.

I need answers on this report before my three o'clock meeting."

I tripped over my own feet, but kept moving for the women's room.

"This is insubordination. I've warned you for the last time, Gabby."

Waving my hand, I called out, "I'm sick," and kept moving. My stomach bounced like a kid in a moonwalk cage. I was sick all right, sick of being bombarded with scenes. Tired of having alternate dimensions or whatever the hell I saw thrust upon me when I least expected. Exhausted from not sleeping worth a damn, and stressed from doing Howie's work and my own. I didn't care if the earth under my feet opened and sucked me down. All I wanted was immediate escape.

Gaining the bathroom, I slammed open the door and made for the nearest stall. I didn't lose my lunch, but it was a near thing. Panting, I leaned against the metal wall and used a wad of toilet paper to wipe my forehead.

What would it take to accomplish the mission I'd never wanted?

Would the craziness never end?

Chapter Thirteen

I left work early and tentatively checked inside my apartment, senses on high alert. My home had been quiet this morning when I left, but the way things were going, I wouldn't take any chances. Cyrano, sprawled on the couch, raised his head and greeted me with a loud meow. All else remained quiet.

Howie had threatened me with a written warning, but my pale face and shaking hands must have convinced him I really didn't feel well. He'd backed off and told me to go home, but not before reminding me I had a report due by nine o'clock the next morning. I wondered what he'd do if I called in sick. Ass wipe.

Life—lives—galloped to a head. I understood Howie's role now and then, and knew leaving the company, whether by choice or termination was a done deal. On the way home, I'd decided to ask Carma about proving who had access to my files and when changes were made. Howie was the kind of guy who'd sabotage me after I was gone. He had me in his sights, and Friday—his favorite day to axe people—came soon.

Donna, who'd come to my bathroom stall rescue with cold cloths and no questions, had railed about my situation during a quick smoke break. Oddly, her anger helped me find calm. Instead of bashing Howie, I accepted I had to take action. Donna thought I should let him fire me then sue for wrongful termination, and maybe I would. Later. First I had to determine how to live without a regular paycheck.

Being fiscally responsible and in spite of the extra outlays I'd made supporting Joel, I had saved enough money to meet my bills for five months without an income. Putting money aside had limited my ability to spend on furniture, clothes and the like. Good thing I'd tightened my belt. But I wouldn't rely on my backup. I'd take time tomorrow updating my resume and printing copies. I figured the firm owed me. Plus, if the company contested my unemployment claim, I'd fight for the money. J&J owed me that, too. No more Ms. Doormat.

A knock sounded. "Gabriella?"

"Door's open."

"Wow. Whatever happened today caused a big swing in your aura. I've never seen it glow so bright."

I gave Chastity a hard hug. "Thanks for being here."

She stepped back, a worried look on her face. "What's happened? And why are you home early?"

"My work computer televised Genevieve's latest life episode, my job is in jeopardy, and I don't give a flying fu…dge. If candy could fly."

Her lips quirked as she registered my quick save. "So you're prepared for anything to happen?"

I considered her statement. "Yeah." My body felt lighter with the pronouncement. "I didn't realize how much of a rut I was in until the weird stuff began. I still don't like visions coming at me with little warning, but I get that life—my life right now—is about being flexible."

"Releasing your attachment to habits, to your

known, is key. Remember that everything your mind throws at you is an illusion. Operating from your heart allows you to change your life, become a different person."

A half-formed smart-ass reflex answer was on my lips, but I forced it down and mulled her woo-woo words. She'd hit the target again. The more comfortable I could be with my strange life, the easier I could move within my fantasy reality.

"Do you remember what I told you about consciousness changing reality?" she asked. "Scientists who observe an experiment with a preconception of how certain particles will react are actually affecting the action. The scientist creates the result he or she desires to happen."

"So what you see is what you get?"

The corners of her mouth tilted up. "You've learned the concept the hard way, now you're on to bigger and better stuff."

"Huh?" I couldn't imagine what she inferred, afraid to take her words at face value.

"You've taken steps, big ones, to change your life. You're letting go of the old stuff, things you thought provided stability. Now you only have to heal your past." Her gaze remained steady on mine. "It's easier than you think. You've already done most of the work. Don't give up now."

"Oh, I meant to tell you. I learned who Howie is, or rather was in my other life." I didn't give her a chance to form the obvious question. "Priscilla. Can you believe?"

"Yes, makes sense." She tapped a fingernail against her hip. "Sometimes souls don't learn the lessons they came here to master. Instead, they get caught up in known behavior."

Given I'd finally made some progress, I didn't want to backslide. "So, how do I keep from falling into my rut?"

"Take the upper hand. Decide what you want and make the first move toward your preferred outcome."

I thought about the first three items of the list I'd previously made.

1. Heal and release my past.

2. Find a new job.

3. Give Adrian a real chance.

Items one and two were in motion and partially out of my control. I could do something about Adrian, though. I had to figure out how to make my move.

Taking a hint from my alternate self, who was about to have dinner with Sheriff Adam, an idea leaped out.

"Why don't you and Mike come over for dinner at six thirty," I said. "And have Mike ask Adrian to join us. I'm in the mood to cook up some trouble."

"Yippee! I'll bring—"

"Yourself Chastity, along with Mike and Adrian. I'll do the rest." I leveled a finger at her. "I mean it. I want to do this."

She sent me a flip salute. "Yes, Ma'am." Turning, she headed for the door. "Consider it done."

Glad I'd done my weekly shopping yesterday, I pulled out the ingredients for Parmesan chicken. I checked my vegetable bin. Fresh veggies and salad makings caught my eye. All I needed was wine and something for dessert and I'd be set.

Step one in my plan to achieve goal number three:

show Adrian I know my way around a kitchen.

I paused. Crap. What the hell was I thinking? Had I really taken on a 1950's how-to-catch-a-guy approach? Next I'd be kneeling at his feet, slipping off his shoes and handing him a pipe and tobacco. Not to mention I'd cooked for Joel and look where that got me.

My body slumped against the counter. The picture outline was not one I wanted to color in, but I had already issued invitations. Knowing Chastity, she'd already called Mike and the date was a done deal. A moment of panic resulted in one main understanding. The problem here was not having friends to dinner but in my intent.

And my intent, while essentially good, was skewed.

Chicken rinsed and patted dry, I considered my situation. Adrian had broadly hinted his interest. He was on my list of what I wanted in my life, and I'd determined to take action. So far, so good.

What I needed to release was my own insecurity, the same insecurity leading me to jump on guys who showed me the least bit of interest. Damn it. I didn't need to trot out my culinary skills or lay myself out on a damn platter for some guy's delectation. Though, admittedly, I wouldn't mind being devoured by Adrian. An image of the kitchen table being put to use in a way not intended by *Good Housekeeping* magazine filled my mind.

Shaking my head, I returned my thoughts to the evolving insights coming my way. Yes, I'd made bad choices in the men department. Yes, I'd attracted some real jerks. I could leave the rut.

Cyrano wound himself around my ankles, purring.

"I've neglected you lately, big boy." He settled in my arms, head butting against my shoulder. "What do you think, sweetie? Should I dig out candles and soft music?"

"Mrowr."

What the heck? Sounded as if Cyrano had replied, "more." I stilled then shook my head. Not possible. "I know I've got candles, but the music might be a bit too much."

He repeated a head butt. "Nwohir."

"No?" My sense of the absurd was intrigued. I continued my feline consultation. "Not too much? So, tell me, Monsieur Cat, shall I don provocative clothes?"

He purred so loud, I jumped. Okay, the scene had passed absurd and moved toward eerie.

"Being the tom cat you are, I guess you'd suggest I change my sheets and put new towels in the bath, too? Maybe dab on perfume?"

"Myrwee."

Mais oui? My cat spoke French? Holy tuna on an ink blot. My imagination ran overtime. I buried my fingers in his fur, rubbing and scratching his favorite spots.

I couldn't deny ending the night in a clinch with Adrian held my imagination. And my sheets needed changing anyway. A blue teddy, sales tags attached had been calling me, wanting out of the drawer. May as well rinse off the memory of Joel, and Howie, and begin anew.

Kissing his head, I placed him on the floor, where he sprawled, his tail flicking. Our gazes met. "Yes, I'll take your advice, Monsieur Cat. You must know your stuff given the number of kittens you've sired in the neighborhood."

He lifted a cat eyebrow and glanced away.

"Thought I didn't know, did you? I'm not sure how you got out, but the cat next door had a litter full of babies looking exactly like you."

Cyrano's concentration appeared to be on licking his paw but his ears were turned in my direction.

"All right, I'll follow your advice, this time. I sure hope you're not leading me astray."

He stood and shook out his feet in a move too overt to miss. "Bwrrah."

"Bring it on? That's your suggestion?"

He glared as if to say, what're you waiting for? "Fine, I'll get a move on." Grabbing my purse, I headed out for wine and dessert. If I hurried, I'd have enough time for housekeeping and a shower. Where the hell had I stashed the candles?

****

"So, have any of the rest of you been having strange dreams lately?" Adrian caught my eye. "Realistic to the point of believing you're in another world? Recognizing people even though they don't appear the same as now?"

His words flew over my head. Dream? Yes, absolutely dreamy with a denim shirt, sleeves rolled back and tight jeans looking washed to softness. When he'd stood at my door offering a bottle of wine, his clean, spicy soap had filled my nostrils and my head with a desire to lick him all over. I'd almost burned the chicken, pulling it from the oven just in time.

Wait a minute. Strange, otherworldly dreams? I dragged my attention from his lips.

"I'd like to hear more," Chastity said.

Of course she would. I wish I knew what she thought. I willed her to look my way, but she remained focused on Adrian.

"Was it one dream or a sequence? And who was in your dream? What happened?" Chastity fired off the questions, and Adrian's fingers tightened around the stem of his wine glass.

He cleared his throat. "Well, I uh, I'm not sure, because I don't remember dreams usually, but this one was so clear. And in an odd way, mirrored tonight." He sipped his wine. "Sort of mirrored, not exactly."

Chastity leaned forward, placing her chin on her palm. "Sounds fascinating. Tell us more."

"Yeah, dude, seeing as how you didn't tell me, your best friend," Mike said. "You've always said you conk out as soon as your head hits the pillow." He snapped his fingers. "Hey, wait. Is this a concept we can use in a game?"

"I wasn't reminded of the dream until just now, and no, I don't think the idea will work for a game. Never mind. It's not important."

Shivers ran down my spine. Whatever he'd experienced needed to be said. "Yes, yes your dream is important," I said. "Tell me, us."

Something in my expression must have convinced him, because after a long look at me, he once again cleared his throat and leaned back in his chair.

"I was in an old-fashioned café, the kind pictured in Westerns, you know, with those boxy print curtains in red and white."

"'Boxy print?' He must mean gingham. My stomach roiled. I had a feeling I knew what he'd say next, because I'd already seen it. "Wooden floors and tables, right?"

He nodded. "Yeah, that kind of stuff. Lanterns. People dressed in old-timey clothes." He canted his head. "I got the impression of heat, but I was more an observer than a participant. Still, I kind of felt warm, like something weighed me down."

"Was there anything special about what you wore?"

He swallowed hard. "Yeah. Apparently, I was some kind of lawman. I wore a badge."

Now I swallowed hard. Waited for what I knew had to come next.

Chastity asked the question I was thinking. "Were you alone or with someone, Adrian?"

He shifted in his chair. "Well, that's the strange thing, what made me think of the dream. Sitting across the table from me was Gabriella. But the café owner called her Genevieve."

I shouldn't have been surprised, but I was. How the hell had Adrian been actively drawn in to my alternate life? Up to now, I thought I'd be the only one observing. Not so, anymore.

My stomach contracted and I put down my fork. Would a swig of wine help me absorb his story? I knew I wouldn't be having dessert unless my gut stopped the rumba.

"We were eating dinner." He flashed a brief grin. "Chicken, but it wasn't boned, flattened and enhanced with herbs, Italian cheese, and white wine." He stared into my eyes. "Still, it was chicken and vegetables, and you were there."

Mike looked intrigued. "Did anything happen at dinner, or did the dream end there?"

"We talked. I walked Gabri, I mean Genevieve, home." He scowled. "Some jerk who reminded me of putzy Joel waited on the street. I was telling him to get lost when the dream ended."

At least I knew how the date ended for Genevieve, but questions dominated my thoughts.

Chastity tilted her head. "So, were you bothered by the dream, or the coincidence of our similar meal?"

"Coincidence" my parallel life. Chastity no more believed in coincidence than I did astrology. Where was she headed?

Adrian studied the tabletop for a moment. Raising his head, he caught my eye, and I fell into his mocha brown gaze.

"The place, the interactions, it all felt real. As real as us sitting here right now. A sort of clarity surrounded the picture, not at all hazy like the few dream images I remember the next day." His fingers pushed his wine glass in small circles before catching my gaze again. "Makes me wonder if you had the same sort of dream."

"I, um—" A double knock sounded at the door. Joel? What could he want?

"You've got guests, you don't need to answer his summons," Chastity said.

She knew who stood outside as well as I did. I shook my head and rose. "May as well get it over with." I opened the door and Joel stepped in without invitation and scanned the room.

"Well, didn't take you long to have Geek Man over for dinner," he sneered.

I tugged on his arm, bringing his attention back. "What do you want, Joel? I told you we were through. So, why the visit?"

"Stopped by to pick up my movies."

I snagged the bag holding his action flicks from my closet and pushed it at him. "Here. Take your explosions, profanity, car chases and go."

His fingers brushed the back of my hand when he took the bag, "What's the matter, Gab? You liked the flicks when we watched them together. Geek Man prefer chick flicks?"

I rubbed my hand to stop the creepy sensation his touch stirred. "No, I'll watch what I prefer from now on, Joel. If the man I date doesn't like my films, he can see the movies he likes on his own. No skin off either nose. And none of your affair."

I threw open the door. "We have no further business with each other, so please leave. If I find any other evidence you were once here, I'll mail it to you."

He stared at me as if I had turned purple with lime green spots.

"Boy, you really have turned into a bossy bitch. Guess I had a lucky escape." He tucked his bag under his arm and swaggered out.

I wanted to swing the door shut in a loud slam, but controlled my impulse. Instead, I clicked the door shut and threw the dead bolt. Turning, I looked Adrian straight in the eyes.

"About the dream. Yes, I've had more than one about you. Maybe we should compare notes, that is, unless you'd rather make a lucky escape?"

"You're the one who got lucky," Adrian said. "The only reason I didn't interfere is because you handled the douche like a champ." He stood and moved closer. "Comparing notes is one activity I'd love to do with you."

Chastity and Mike scraped back their chairs and jumped to their feet. "Thanks for dinner, Gabriella," they chimed in unison.

"But we haven't had dessert," I said. I hoped they hadn't noted my half-hearted objection.

"Mike and I will have something next door. Besides, you know my stance on white sugar."

I couldn't pass up the opportunity to rag on her. "Admit it. You think white sugar is the devil's tool." Heating up our well-worn argument to ignore my sudden nerves, I continued. "There's tons of sugar in chocolate. Cocoa." I squinted toward the ceiling, my head back. "Moderation, Chastity. Everything, even sugar, is good in moderation."

She and Mike exchanged a heated look. "Not everything," she murmured.

Unlocking and opening the door, I watched them dance out. Adrian moved behind me, clasping his hands on my upper arms.

"Are you sure about your stance on moderation?"

His low, intimate tone caused chill bumps on my neck. My muscles relaxed.

"Because I'd like to share dessert with you, and I aim to eat my fill." He kissed the soft area behind my ear. "A nibble here." He nipped at my ear lobe. "A nibble there." His lips moved to my neck. "And once I've finished a serving, I'll be looking for seconds. I'm a glutton."

My knees wobbled. Heat moved down my body in a flash. Adrian continued his attentions, and only his grip on my arms kept me from having my way with him. "I thought you wanted to compare notes on dreams?"

"I think talking about dreams is best in bed. How about you?"

Good thing my apartment is small, my bedroom mere steps away. Had I been given time to think, I may not have made a move. I tugged on his hand. "This way to my dream laboratory."

Chapter Fourteen

Cyrano looked up from his nest in the middle of the bed. He stretched and jumped off, tail held high as he hurried from the room trying to appear casual.

Even though I have no animal communication skills, I could easily read the look on his face. The "about time" stare as he passed needed little interpretation.

Adrian embraced me from behind. His arms enfolded me with heat and a sense of security. "Now about dessert," he said, kissing behind my ear. "What did you have in mind?"

I stilled, quickly taking stock of my emotions, believing if I had any doubts, Adrian would cease and desist. That certainty helped me decide. I wrapped my hands around his thighs. Well, what I could wrap. The man has some strong legs.

He moved his lips to the nape of my neck. "I could go for a bite of pie." He nipped lightly before laving the area.

His arms tightened around me. I felt his erection against my buttocks. "Or maybe fresh fruit. Cherries. Bananas. Together. Creating juices."

He flexed his hips against me, his hands covering my breasts. "Peaches, too. Let's not forget the peaches."

Sudden heat enveloped me. My mouth dried even

though any mention of food normally made me salivate. I rested my head against his shoulder, allowing his hands free reign. He took the hint and covered my mound with one hand, rubbing me through my slacks.

"Pudding? Will you serve me a sweet, moist pudding?" He moved to the crook of my neck, leaving an open-mouthed kiss there. One hand continued to caress my breasts while the other kept up a circular rubbing motion below. Nudging aside my lightweight blouse with his chin, he feathered kisses along my shoulder blades.

"Then there's cake," he lightly breathed the words against my skin. "Rich, dark chocolate layers divided by ganache."

His ministrations affected me like spark to tinder. I pushed my ass against his groin, arching with pleasure.

"So, what do you offer this evening?"

Finally, I pulled together words, though my voice rasped. "I, uh, have a tray of tiramisu from Mancini's."

"Ah, you temptress." He'd unzipped my slacks and inserted his hand inside my teddy. "The recipe for tiramisu is ladyfingers soaked," now he inserted one finger into my hot, wet vagina. "Soaked, ah, god."

Turning my head, I noticed his ear was within range, so I nipped then sucked on his lobe. His mouth captured mine. Our tongues met and danced. When he lifted away, he panted and kissed my temple. I felt surrounded by pleasure and heat, his hands increasing pressure while his growing erection rubbed against my crack. I writhed against him like a cat in heat.

"Where was I?" he murmured. "Ah, yes, soaked fingers. What else makes up tiramisu?" He rolled a nipple between his fingers while his finger moved inside me. I reached behind us, running my hands over his tight buttocks.

"Espresso," I said in a breathy voice. "For stamina." My head rolled against his shoulders and heat traveled my body. "Because I'm not sure I can hold out for long."

"So let go," he murmured. "This is all about you."

"Not yet. Not while we're building dessert."

"Hmm. I do like anticipation." He licked my ear lobe then pulled it between his teeth. "We can't forget the rum. Because you intoxicate me."

His deep voice filled my center as did the second finger he'd added to the first. My inner walls dripped. "Ah, god, what you're doing."

"Me? You're the one doing the work." I went up on tiptoes as his fingers pushed in. My breasts strained for release, the teddy's silk abrading my nipples. I was caught, trapped by my clothes and surrounded with Adrian's heat.

He flexed his hips, his erection strong against my back while his hands picked me apart. "I know what we're missing." His hot breath wafted over my ear. "One more ingredient." The fingers of one hand moved inside me with urgent rhythm. Pulling the teddy off my shoulder, he licked his other fingers and massaged my nipples. A jolt of energy ran from my breast to my inner core. My hips rolled and I couldn't, didn't want to control my moans.

My knees turned to jelly. Adrian moved from caressing my breasts to supporting me by pressing me against him at my stomach. My head rolled from side to side.

"Ah, how could I forget the best part, creamy

mascarpone." He lightly massaged my trigger. His move from filling me to focusing on one small but vital and sensitive point had me craving more.

His tongue circled my outer ear. "Come for me," he breathed. "Let go. Say yes."

Pressure built behind my eyes and in my womb. I felt an orgasm hovering. He pushed his fingers in while his thumb circled and pressed against my mound. My hips rotated and thrust. My heart beat faster, quicker than the moans filling my bedroom. I thought my body would levitate.

Then he stopped all movement but for lightly rubbing my clitoris. The pinpointed attention pushed me over the edge with an enthusiastic shout of "Yes!" I came around his fingers, my inner walls gripping him in recurring spasms.

He remained curved around me, kissing my neck as I fell apart. "I think tiramisu has moved to the top of my all-time favorite desserts," he said, his voice hoarse.

"If you give me a minute to recover, I'll show you how a banana split may change your mind."

He guided me to the bed, following after as he eased me down. "I want to worship you all night."

I rubbed his rock hard penis. "But it's your turn."

"Later." Catching my hands, he pushed them above my head. "Let me show you why I believe you're a goddess. Someone to adore."

"You've given me an orgasm I won't ever forget. I'd like to return the favor."

He crossed my lips with his forefinger. "Shh. Lie back and relax. You deserve what I was in too much of a hurry to give you earlier. Total adoration."

I squirmed and reached for him. "I don't—"

"You do." His eyes darkened and he intercepted my questing hands. Kissing my knuckles, he pinned my arms above my head. "I meant what I said. I'm your acolyte."

Promise shown in his expression along with a plea for trust. I gulped and nodded.

"First, much as I like the color blue, I'd rather be looking at your pink skin. Let's get this piece of total temptation off you." He suited action to words, gently easing off my no longer brand new teddy. His fingers rubbed the material and my mouth went dry with recent memory.

"What about you? I'd like a look, too."

"I follow the wishes of my goddess." He stood and stripped without removing his gaze from mine.

Lost in his eyes, I almost forgot to watch as his toned body was revealed with every discarded piece of clothing. He looked down to untie and pull off his shoes, and I grabbed the opportunity to examine him.

Holy Hard Body. He wasn't a gym rat with muscles on top of muscles and no neck, a fact I applauded. Broad shoulders and strong arms, yes. Light chest hair. Yowsa. A flat stomach? Check. He bent to tug off jeans bunched at his ankles, showing off a fine and firm ass. I liked that his moves were a little clumsy instead of smooth and polished. Tugging off his jeans, he revealed sturdy legs with defined muscles, and a package qualifying as stellar in my book.

He stood at ease, arms at his sides. "Do I meet with your approval?"

"Absolutely. Approval plus." I patted the bed.

He accepted my non-verbal invitation and slid in beside me. "I want to kiss you all over." He sat up. "In fact, I won't wait. Get ready to be adored."

Nerves hit my stomach. I cleared my throat. "Um, I thought we would um, you know."

He didn't answer but slid to my feet. His dark gaze met mine. "Later." Grasping one foot in his hands, he began massaging the sole. Rubbing the arch. Nibbling at my toes before sucking them into his mouth. Sending my nerves but not my reluctance, to perdition. He ministered to the other foot, moving his way up my body one section at a time. Carefully avoiding my genitals, and in the process, increasing the relaxed buzzing sensation he created with every touch.

Although tense at first, his gentle touch eventually won me over, right about at my hips, or maybe my stomach. I could stand to lose about ten pounds, and five of those are at my stomach and hips. When Adrian first swiped his hand over my pooch, I winced. Here's where his touch would falter, his adoration become abhorrence. When, instead, his lips and tongue made brief love to my navel, I caught a glimpse of what unconditional love must be like.

His hands spanned my ribs and I knew no one could adore me unless I allowed them. As Adrian planted a kiss above my heart, my palms covered his jaw and cheeks. Our kiss was gentle yet passionate, given without tongue.

He lifted away, supporting himself with his forearms. "Now do you understand how special you are?"

I nodded, willing the tears welling in my eyes not to fall. My throat felt sandy.

"I wanted you to understand before we make love, really make love, for the first time."

"May I return the favor?" My voice sounded hoarse, but we both heard the entreaty.

"With pleasure. Later." He unwrapped and sheathed himself with a condom. Then he settled himself between my legs and, holding my gaze with his, entered with one smooth push.

I don't know whether his ministrations had made me super sensitive or if I hadn't yet experienced all the aftershocks of my previous orgasm, but my body lit like he'd thrown a transformer switch. I hummed in all the right places.

"Oh, Christ. You're so wet, so hot. I'm losing my fucking head." He gasped and plunged. "Both of them."

I planted my heels on the mattress, lifting and meeting his thrusts. The sounds of wet sucking filled the air. Lacing his fingers with mine, he pushed our joined hands against the bed. He left open-mouthed kisses against my neck and shoulders. I kissed any nearby body part. My awareness concentrated on our joining, the thrust and parry of hips.

"I'm sorry. I can't—"

He gave an inarticulate cry and several hard pumps. His pulsing triggered my release, and I followed him into the maelstrom. We clung and panted, sweat coated our bodies.

My pulse pounded. I wasn't accustomed to having two mind-blowing orgasms so close together. Or ever. Until tonight.

I drifted off, content within Adrian's embrace. I could get used to this goddess stuff.

Chapter Fifteen

Genevieve opened the door of Mrs. Maddox's home. Adam stood before her, hat in hands.

"Genevieve, I…I've come to tell you good-bye."

Her jaw dropped. "Good-bye?" She swallowed. "You're coming back aren't you?"

"I hope so." He pointed to his chest, where the sheriff star no longer hung. "Not sure I'll have a job when I get back, but I'm drawn to my duty. My real duty."

"I…don't…understand. Real duty? You aren't joining up, are you? The town needs a sheriff more than the CSA needs you."

He looked pained. "May I come in? I'd rather speak in private."

She stood back. "Of course. My apologies. Would you like a cup of coffee? Fresh apple pie?"

He led her into the living room and shut the door. Turning, he set down his hat and took her hands in his. "I'm hoping you won't hate me, Miss Genevieve."

Her posture tightened. "Hate you? Why, what have you done? It's not Jeb, is it? Did you arrest him?" Her hand covered her mouth. "Did you kill him and now you must leave?"

He placed a finger over her lips. "No, but it'd be worth your safety if anyone overheard my plans."

Genevieve's expression held confusion and fear. "I

don't understand."

"I've got to do what I think is correct." His forehead creased. "This war. It's not right."

Her expression switched to comprehension. "You're signing up, but not in the Confederate Army."

"I'd rather not say, if you don't mind."

"The truth is written on your face, Adam."

He grabbed her hands. "Please don't hate me."

"Why are you repeating those words? I could no more hate you than the sun hates the moon for taking the sky over at night. You're a man of honor, and as such, must follow his beliefs. I'm sorry we aren't on the same side, but I understand. God knows this is a hateful war, with family fighting family, and for nothing more than greed."

"A bit more than greed, I'd say, when people are stolen and sold as slaves. Mistreated. I can't uphold the law here. Not when it means defending a system I don't believe in." He placed his hands on her shoulders. "I'm not here to talk about laws or right and wrong. I have something for you."

Reaching into his jacket, he pulled out a sheaf of papers. "These are for you."

She continued watching him, her face reflecting sorrow. She glanced at the packet but made no move. "What are those?"

"Title to my property. Everything I have, it's all yours free and clear."

"I can't accept such a gift. We aren't betrothed much less married."

"If I didn't have to leave this afternoon, I'd take care of that matter. As it is, Judge O'Connor prepared the papers. It's all legal." He pushed the packet at her.

"Take this gift, please. You left your home because of the conflict between your brother and myself. The least I can do is ensure your future."

"But your family?"

"Don't need the land. I want to give you this part of me." He placed his hands on her shoulders, the papers falling to the floor. "I love you. You're all I have, all I want. If I come back—"

"When," she said, all but shouting.

He smiled. "When I return, we'll be married and farm the land together. I've got a running stream, and enough flat land for crops. Plenty of trees for our kids to climb."

Her palm caressed his jaw. "Don't go."

He ran his fingers through his hair. "I must. Don't you see? The law of our country is as important as enforcing the town's rules."

She grasped his hands. "Let's marry and move up there now."

"Sweetheart, I wish we could, but I need to take care of this other matter first."

"I appreciate your sense of honor. I can't stand in your way, though I wish I could." A tiny smile flickered on her face. "You have the darnedest way of proposing, Adam."

He grinned. "I do, don't I? So you will marry me? Be my love?"

"I'll be your love no matter what, Adam. Don't think you can escape me so easily. I'm a woman of means, now. You couldn't do better if you looked all over the South."

"The only thing I'll be looking for is the earliest opportunity to be with you." He covered her lips with

153

his. "Even if we never see each other again, I'll look for you through eternity."

I woke in a flash, my chest heaving. My gaze scanned the room as I attempted to focus on where I was and when. Sunlight invaded through a crack in the drapes.

Adrian lay beside me with eyes wide open. His face was pale. He gripped my fingers.

"What's wrong?"

"I had one of those dreams," he said. "From long ago. Civil War times." He brushed hair from my forehead. "You were there."

Did I tell him his dream wasn't a dream? Even though I'd been experiencing alternate dimensions for a while, now, I still wasn't comfortable with the idea, and no way could I explain the mechanics. I opted for the easy way out. "Tell me."

As he described the first part of his dream, I recognized it matched mine, only told from his viewpoint. Then he described what happened after Adam left Genevieve and my hands chilled despite his warmth.

"You know how dreams jump around? Well, I remember leaving the house, but suddenly I was on my horse riding through the woods. I had the feeling someone followed me, but they must have been hiding in the trees."

"What happened next?"

"The dream hopped again and I lay on the ground, my shoulder on fire. I'd been shot. No sign of my horse." He ran his hand through his hair. "I remember looking into the barrel of a gun then I woke up." He laughed but the sound shook. "Guess it was a good thing I woke up, huh?"

"I'll say." I laid my hand on his chest and felt his racing heartbeat. "You're here now." I kissed his chin. "With me."

No wonder I'd had a feeling Adrian couldn't be trusted. Now I understood the feeling I'd had was not mistrust, but abandonment. Sheriff Adam had ridden off, not to war, but to an ambush. While he hadn't seen the shooter, or at least not admitted to an identity, my gut told me it had to have been someone from town. Someone who knew Adam's enlistment plans and didn't wait for a battlefield.

I struggled to make sense of this insight while fighting a sense of doom. Were we slated to repeat the past, or could we avoid our mistakes? I wasn't sure.

"Strange dream, huh? You didn't have a weird dream, I hope."

"Actually, I did." Gnawing my lower lip, I answered slowly. "I had the same dream, right up to when you left."

"The same?"

I nodded.

"Wow."

"Yeah, and there's more, if Chastity is right. She thinks these aren't dreams but alternate lives."

He closed his eyes in thought. "Actually makes a sort of sense. According to Einstein, time and space are linked. Others believe the universe continues inflating, like a giant inhalation. Mike and I have been brainstorming a new game featuring dimension jumps between levels." He palm slapped his forehead. "Now I know where he got the idea."

He propped himself on his elbow and grinned at

me. "I don't want to talk science with a gorgeous naked woman lying beside me."

"It's not theory when a person experiences something, is it?"

His expression turned serious. "No, it's not, and how long have you been dreaming about this other life of yours, ours?"

"Several weeks."

"And you've figured out all the players?"

I nodded.

"So?"

"So it's the past. Let's forget about it." Cyrano jumped on the bed, circled twice, and curled up next to Adrian's knees, the opposite of his normal loud meows demanding food. Traitor.

"Time to feed Cyrano and get ready for work. Would you like breakfast?"

"Are you trying to get rid of me? You told me you work from home on Thursday morning," he said.

"Yeah, well, Howie put the kibosh on my arrangement yesterday. Said he wanted me where he could see I was working. Ass-wipe. He piles on his duties then keeps calling me into his office on a whim. I can barely move as it is."

"Why don't you give him the kiss-off? You're smart. You should be working somewhere you're appreciated."

"Oh, right," I snorted. "Like employers are waiting in line."

He sat and grabbed my shoulders. "They would be if you'd stop running yourself down. You're bright, organized, and loyal. Any employer would love to have you. All you have to do is show them the real you."

His words hurt, mostly because I knew he spoke the truth. Hadn't I come to terms with my own worst behavior before dinner last night? Still, it hurt to hear a relative stranger—for all we'd been intimate—tell me I lacked something, anything in his eyes.

"Right, like you know me so well."

His expression shuttered. "I think I can see your good points, even if you won't admit them."

"Oh, really."

He nodded. "In fact, Mike and I need someone to organize our office. Our last job, well, we're moving into the big leagues. We need someone we can trust to handle our books, taxes, other stuff."

My palm smoothed his cheek. "Your offer is sweet." I dropped my hand. "But one client won't pay my bills." Ignoring the very real temptation of his bare chest, I moved to rise.

He put his hand on my upper arm. "I haven't told you what we'll pay. The office is a mess. It'll take a high-powered person to straighten everything out. We know it'll cost." He pulled me close. "Besides, if we live together, you won't have many bills. Unless you want to split everything down the middle, but that's not necessary. I have enough money to support us both."

My heart stopped. Yes, I know it's physically impossible, but I know what I felt. Nothing. No beat. No blood moving through my veins. The whole damn world, including my aorta, froze.

"What did you say?"

He cupped the back of my head in his hand, and enormous pupils engulfed his gaze. "Move in with me. Let me take care of you, give you an opportunity to establish your business without having money worries."

My heart started-up, triple time, as if to make up for having quit. My lungs seized and my pulse raced. He couldn't be serious. "This isn't the 1860's you know. Besides, writing a computer game can't bring in anywhere near enough money."

"It's a sideline, now a lucrative one. We also write phone apps, consult on and design network security and phone systems. Living in a small town doesn't mean we aren't big time. In our own small way."

He cocked his head. "We both know there's a link, a strong one between us. Why waste time?" His gaze turned inward. "Life is too damn short." He shook his head. "Didn't take a scary ass dream to pound the point home, but I'm not walking out of here without an answer. Are you willing to act on our connection? Make the choice leading to happiness? Or will you stay stuck in your quagmire of fear?" He dropped his hand from my head. "Up to you."

My thoughts spun. I looked from Adrian to Cyrano and back. My throat closed. "Do I have to make my choice right now? Can't I have time to think?"

His pupils contracted. "So you don't feel like I do? I thought we had a lot in common."

"Having similar beliefs doesn't mean we must agree on everything."

His lips turned down at the corners. "I guess."

"Go ahead and finish what you were going to add after the unsaid "but.""

His jaw tightened. "I guess I've learned when a woman says she wants time to think, it's an excuse to say "no" later on. Why not turn me down up front?"

"Excuse me? I don't like getting painted with the "all women are alike" brush, thank you very much. If I say I need time, I need time."

"Guess your feelings and mine aren't as in sync as I'd thought. I go after what I want first and think second. Primitive, I know." He moved Cyrano from against his knees and moved off the bed. "I'll get going. Give you space."

While his tone hadn't devolved into a sneer, I sensed his anger and disappointment. His emotions matched mine, but my throat was too tight to push words out.

Trust me to turn a night to remember into the dawn from hell. I ran into the bathroom to hide the welling tears. When I came out, the apartment was empty.

****

"Come to my office, now." Howie hung up before I could even get out a "hello." I grabbed my recorder, file folder and pad of paper then headed for his office. This meeting was simply the icing on the crap cake I'd baked earlier this morning.

After Adrian had walked out, Cyrano had turned his back on me. He hadn't come when I'd opened a can of tuna, hadn't even looked my way when I'd called "good-bye" before shutting the door. Yeah, I existed in kitty purgatory, and I wasn't sure I'd ever earn the right to return.

The defection of both the man I cared for and my cat left me feeling fragile and on edge. If I didn't keep an extra tight lid on my emotions, I'd say or do something I couldn't call back.

"You wanted to see me?"

Howie didn't even glance my way. "Come in and close the door behind you."

I followed his instructions and stood before his

desk.

"You can sit down, but you won't be staying long."

"Are you assigning a new report, or is something else on your mind?"

"Something else." His close-mouthed smile reminded me of a sly three-year-old. "I'm letting you go."

I blinked. Even knowing he'd been building this confrontation didn't make the moment easier. "I'm sorry. What did you say?"

"You're fired. Terminated. Canned. Whatever word you prefer. Pack your personal effects and leave. Security will escort you out, so don't try to take anything you didn't bring here."

My emotional status, already on edge from my fight with Adrian, tipped into the danger zone. "That's it?" My voice rose. "You aren't even giving me a reason? You can't do this."

He showed his teeth. "Actually, I can. North Carolina is an "at-will" employment state." He rubbed his hand across his mouth. "You want reasons? Okay, fine. You were late again this morning. Your insubordination has worsened. The reports I've assigned are done last minute. Enough reasons for you? I'm kicking you to the curb."

His recitation hadn't helped. I still couldn't take in the scene. "But I've worked here for years and have always had positive evaluations. Bonuses."

"Until recently, yes." He examined his fingernails then looked up with a hard stare. "Unfortunately, your work has slipped. You no longer produce, and this company is all about maximizing production and benefits. Besides, you have an unprofessional attitude."

I lost it. I didn't even try to keep a grip. "Then why the hell have they kept you on? I've been doing the majority of your work for months."

"Tut. There's the unprofessional attitude I mentioned. No respect for authority."

"Authority? You consider yourself a leader, you, you worm? You're damn right I don't respect you. If I hadn't needed this job, I'd have laughed in your face and left like most the rest of the staff has, you jerk off. Do you think anyone here has missed seeing you with your men's magazines? Your hurried trips to the bathroom? Really? And don't get me started on the down-loaded racing forms."

He stood and I jumped to my feet so he couldn't lean over me. "Get out," he snarled.

"Not before I finish my say. " I stuck my finger in his face. "Don't even try messing with my reputation or my unemployment claim. Believe me. You don't know what you've started."

I slammed out of his office and marched to my desk. Donna stood in the aisle between the cubicles, her face white. I shook my head, letting her know she needed to keep her distance. We both knew I'd call her as soon as I left the building.

A cardboard box waited on my desk. I slipped the recorder in, leaving it running. Then I filled the box, making sure I palmed the drive holding my spreadsheet on Howie. I had a duplicate at home, but didn't want to leave anything giving my actions away. At first, I tossed my achievement certificates in the trash, then reconsidered and added them to my box.

"Whoever wants my plants can have them," I announced to the room. "I'm outta here. Good luck, you guys. You deserve better than the boss you have."

One of the security guards, a new employee whose hands shook with nerves, stepped forward to either hustle me out or take my box. I wasn't sure which.

"Sorry. I'll leave quietly." And I did, though I wanted to throw my monitor at Howie's head.

When I walked outside, the sun was shining, the sky a deep blue found only, I think, in Carolina in the autumn. I walked a block, spotted an empty bench and sank down, box at my feet.

Talk about a flame out. I pulled my phone from the bottom of my purse and dialed Donna. When she didn't answer, I assumed she'd either been called before Howie or she was in a meeting. Didn't matter. I'd catch up with her later.

The acid in my stomach could have eaten through industrial strength powder-coated steel. Sure, I had enough money to live quietly until I found something else in town, but what? Howie was the kind of guy who'd backstab me in a flash. He'd probably got on the phone before I left the building, calling around to all his friends to ensure I couldn't get hired.

I slumped against the back of the bench. Now what?

"Well, what's the problem, Sweetcakes? Nerd Boy send you packing? Told ya."

My shoulders tensed. Hell, my whole body turned into one of those spring-loaded abdominal exerciser machines impossible to use unless you already had developed muscles. Fricking Joel. Next to him, wearing an identical smirk, Red Dress Woman from the restaurant.

I stood. "Joel. I'd say it was nice to see you again

but you know my stand on honesty."

He put his arm over his companion's shoulders. "I've got a real woman now, so don't come crying. I won't answer the door."

"The only thing I want from you, Joel, is the money you borrowed and never returned. You signed a note remember? Due at the end of this month?"

I studied his suddenly pale complexion. "Maybe your new woman will give you the cash."

Catching her eye I said, "Honey, I'm gonna give you complete disclosure. Joel's a user. I know he's handsome with a sexy body, but pretty is doesn't mean pretty does. If you lend him money, make him sign loan papers."

He pulled his companion in the opposite direction from me.

"So long, Joel. Pay me back by the due date or I'll see you in court!"

I sank onto the bench, oddly cheered by the encounter. As long as I was crashing and burning, I may as well make the descent spectacular.

Chapter Sixteen

Cyrano had gotten over his snit when I arrived home. Either that, or we're linked telepathically and he'd decided to cut me a break given my day. He ran when I opened the door and wrapped his body around my ankles, purring loud enough for Chastity to stick her head out her apartment door.

"Gabriella? What are you doing home early *again*?"

"I'm home for good. Howie fired my ass this morning."

"What?" She stepped into the hall.

"Yeah, then I saw Joel and his new girlfriend."

She pulled me into a hug. Her face glowed. Obviously, Mike agreed with her.

"You need a hot drink. Perhaps detox tea to clear your vibes," Leaning back, she scanned me from head to toe. "Though I must say, your aura is vibrant. I never would have guessed you'd had two traumatic experiences this morning."

I grinned. "Maybe because I told both men off. Big time." I grabbed her wrist and pulled her into my apartment.

"Wait, let me close my door." She dashed out and returned before I had deposited my box of belongings on the closet floor. "So tell me, *what happened*?"

We settled on my couch with Cyrano between us. I

related the story, telling her about my spreadsheet and voice recordings, a secret I'd held from everyone even Donna.

"Well, sweetie. You know this opens you up for the job with Mike and Adrian." Her eyebrows rose. "Don't tell me you weren't aware they want to hire you?"

I folded my fidgeting hands together. "I um, thought Adrian was bull shi…rather, hadn't checked with Mike. So, I, ah, turned him down."

"You refused an offer to start your own firm. One you've dreamed of and planned."

I huffed. "Well, I thought the price was too high."

"I don't understand. I'm sure salary is negotiable. Their business is doing very well. And you know I'd help you if you needed investment capital."

"That's not it," I said, shaking my head. "Adrian asked me to live with him."

She crowed—yes, crowed—and clapped her hands. "But that's wonderful!"

I leaned against the sofa back and closed my eyes. "It would be wonderful if I hadn't freaked out. Said no way Jose."

Her eyebrows met above her nose. "You used those words?"

"I may as well have."

"Why?"

I inhaled through my nose, happy she hadn't walked out on me in a snit. Her defection would have sent me over the thin edge of reason—not a long trip. "Because of the dream we shared and because I'm a scared rabbit of a person." I'd figured that much and more out on my walk home.

"A shared dream? Do you want to tell me?"

Nodding, I related both my vision and Adrian's.

"Your sexual intimacy established the final link, allowing you both to learn of the past during this lifetime. That's a precious gift."

"Why? Do you know something pertinent?"

"Each life is an opportunity to grow through the issues we set for ourselves. Our lessons," she said.

"What if Adrian leaves me again? Will I have failed my lessons?" My stomach was tied in knots. "He was killed." A scream built in my chest. "I couldn't stand a repeat."

"Humans have killed and been killed since we came to this planet. You don't know why Adam was shot, but I assure you there is a cosmic balance at work. What happened in one life doesn't necessarily have to occur again. We have choices."

"I understand on an intellectual level, but not emotionally," I said. "This is a big deal."

"Yes, and this is your opportunity for healing."

My heart told me she was right. I had to make a conscious choice and release what happened in my other life. I wasn't the one who pulled the trigger. And while I was certain Jebediah killed Adam, I couldn't have stopped him then. If, indeed the fatal shot was taken in the parallel life. My knowledge of how all this cosmic stuff worked remained iffy.

"Ask yourself why this situation means so much. What emotions are at play?"

My pulse stuttered. That's when everything snapped into place. My angst had more to do with the strong feelings I had for Adrian than with guilt.

Adrian reported seeing a gun barrel and I flipped

out. Criminy. Though I'd been moving around in space and time, I was no physicist. Neither was I a space cadet, unless it came to denying my feelings for Adrian.

The man was important to my wellbeing. I could breathe and live without him, but a big part of my heart would be missing. Didn't matter we hadn't known each other long in our current life. Not when we had so much shared history. If he were hurt physically, I'd feel the pain. My emotional dismay over our earlier argument was proof.

Once again, or maybe still, I was in love with Adrian Comstock. He'd been my past partner, he'd returned, and would again in the future.

My choice would ripple through time, or space, or whatever makes up the way our lives unfold. I'd made plenty of bad decisions, but I'd also made a bunch of good ones. The resolution to trust and love who I am no matter how I screw up—and I knew I'd continue evolving—meant I could find peace.

Trusting myself was worth the price I'd paid and would pay. I was damn worth the effort. So was my love for Adrian.

"So, now you've returned to the room, what will you do next?"

I took a deep breath, looked her in the eyes, and spoke the truth. "First, I have an important project. Then I need a plan so Adrian will listen."

Chastity's face lit up with a huge grin. "You go, girl."

"Now I feel like a bad friend, dumping on you and not asking about you and Mike."

"I didn't want to say anything earlier, but I've given notice on my apartment. We're moving in together." She squeezed my hand. "Girlfriend, *he's The One*."

I stifled my dismay at losing my neighbor and smiled. "I'm so glad for you both!"

She jumped to her feet and began singing the lyrics to "Ain't No Stopping Us Now." She was no McFadden & Whitehead, but she had the groove down, her kimono billowing as she executed a disco turn.

I joined her. Fake it till you make it and all that.

****

"Carma? This is Gabby. I don't know if you can speak, but—"

"But nothing. You are the woman of the hour. Hell, the year. I'm so glad I had a ringside seat for your confrontation, even if I couldn't hear the words. His face turned puce. I'd hoped I'd see his head explode like a cartoon character, but no luck. He looked like one pissed-off dude."

"That's why I called. Can you tell me about the J&J file backup system? Is it possible for Howie to change data? Sabotage my work?"

"If he tries, I'll find his tracks. Believe me."

"Whew," I said.

"Don't worry. We've got your back." She sucked a breath. "Speaking of Satan, gotta run. Hang in there, kiddo."

I shook my fear about Howie appearing in Carma's department. He probably wanted to ensure my computer access was cancelled and to spread his side of my termination story.

I hung up and burned a copy of my voice recordings. Then, I printcd out the spreadsheet report detailing Howie interactions. While I wasn't sure whether recordings made without his permission could be used as evidence in North Carolina, at least I had some verbal backup for my story. Before I could question my resolve, I made an appointment for the following week with a local attorney who specializes in unlawful dismissal suits.

Finally, I phoned the Unemployment Office for information on filing, though everything I am resisted the call. Knowing I'd be hurting for money sooner than later if I couldn't find work helped me leave my pride behind. I'd done two people's work and gotten fired anyway. Nothing to be ashamed about there.

I'd no sooner hung up than Donna's number flashed on my phone's screen.

"You're answering," Donna said. "Good. I have news."

"You've quit and you're starting your own company? You'll be hiring me?"

"Close but not quite. I pulled my head from the sand and requested a meeting with Mr. Jackson."

"Which one?"

"Malachi. The one who thinks he handles human resources."

I caught my breath. "And?"

"He's scrutinizing your termination."

"Yeah, well, thanks for raising a stink, but I'm worried you'll find yourself out on the street, too." Donna had more expenses than me, and I suspected she didn't have much in savings.

Her laugh echoed over the line. "He's called a freeze on Howie's employment actions. Mr. Jackson said he'd done nothing but hire replacements lately. From now on, Howie has to run every employment decision past Malachi."

A good change but a little too late. "Yippee!" I even sounded sincere.

"No shit. Carma hinted you might have a secret. Something you've been doing without telling me?"

My face heated. Good thing she couldn't see me. "Yeah, well, I didn't want to put you at jeopardy." I sucked in a breath. "Carma fed me correct report data so I could compare with Howie's numbers. I'd get advance information giving me prep time."

"You didn't need to hide your actions from me." Donna clipped off the words.

"I knew I could trust you, but Carma asked me to keep her actions quiet."

"I understand," she said. "She should really have channeled everything through the department manager."

"Exactly." I told her the rest. "Besides the data I have voice recordings of meetings with Howie. A spreadsheet of our interactions and a log recording all the work he pushed onto me."

"Girl, you are telling me what I wanted to hear. Mind giving me a copy?"

"Donna, no. I don't want you fighting my battles. I've got an appointment with an attorney for next week."

"Good. I'll trade you. Your stuff for Carma's. She said besides the favor she'd done you—though she wouldn't explain said favor—you might like a report detailing Howie's Internet history."

"What did it show?"

"Howie spends more time betting on line than working."

"Not surprised," I said. "Tell Carma I appreciate her thinking of me." I sighed. "I doubt the information will mean much in a family run firm."

"You've forgotten the recent memo about Internet usage. Plus, there's no love lost in that Jackson family. Malachi said Howie was born a liar and cheat and mumbled something about Howie's father and sandbox toys."

A previously ignored puzzle piece clicked into place. "Malachi? You're calling a VP by his first name?"

"He insisted."

"Huh."

"Not important Gabby. I have a meeting with him tomorrow morning. If you'd agree to give me copies of your documentation, I think your logs would go a long way toward some real changes in the department."

No brainer—helping Donna and my ex-coworkers? Absolutely. J&J would find out soon enough that I'd been keeping records if the attorney took my case. Perhaps the threat of a lawsuit would create change faster than the actual litigation could.

"I'll do it. You can have my back-up thumb drive. Where should I meet you?"

We agreed on a time and place and hung up.

An image of Madame LaMere appeared in my mind's eye. I felt an overwhelming urge to speak with her. Her storefront may or may not be real, but what did I have to lose by checking?

****

Today no crisp wind sent leaves skittering around my feet, and the hole-in-the-wall restaurant at the end of Madame L.'s alley hadn't yet opened.

I tried to ignore the hair on my nape standing up as I moved closer to her store. If Madame L. even existed, would she be available? She may have someone already with her. Then what? I knew I couldn't leave without answers, but the very real fear I'd never find her thrummed through my veins.

When I saw Madame LaMere's painted window and the deep purple door decorated with gold stars, I inhaled deeply. I didn't get dizzy with the renewed oxygen, but my head spun for a quick moment. Thank heavens her shop stood where I expected. This time, I wasn't surprised. I figured her store came and went, transported through the vagaries of time to those who needed her. Kind of like *Dr. Who's* Tardis. I opened the door, listening for the tiny bell signaling arrival.

Once again, the small room stood empty but for two straight-backed chairs and a scratched end table. "Madame LaMere?"

She pushed quietly into the room. Today she wore a multi-hued skirt and white blouse topped by a velvet jacket. Multiple necklaces hung in varied lengths.

"Ah, welcome back Gabriella."

Madame L. motioned me behind the curtain and I followed. Her gray tiger-striped cat watched me through narrowed eyes but didn't move from her cushion.

"I see you have stepped onto the bridge of change. In fact, you are but several steps from reaching the other side. Why have you stalled?"

"I don't know how to proceed."

She leveled me with a look and a raised eyebrow. "Do you not?"

"Okay, fine. Do you want to hear my story or do

you already know?"

Her lips quirked. "You have chosen to return. What is said here is also your choice. You decide what is important."

"Adrian," burst from me before I could censor myself. "Adrian Comstock, the man you told me about, is important and I sent him away. He may never return."

"So you now accept he is your true love? And you are willing to complete healing the pivotal timeline?"

"Finish healing? I thought I had done everything."

"Tsk. Would you remain standing on the bridge had you finished? I think not." She waved her hand as if shooing a fly. "Do you recall me saying your insecurities and anger would hamper you? That you must heal not only your own life but the ones of those who touch you most closely?"

"Yes, vaguely."

Madame L. looked to the ceiling. "Why do you send me people who don't want to listen and do the work?"

I checked the ceiling but saw only plaster.

She sighed. "Once again. You must act from your heart."

"I want to act from my heart but—"

"But you are unsure what action to take. You want direction. Guidelines."

I nodded. "Yes."

"You do not want these things from me."

"I don't?"

She shook her head. "What action does your heart suggest?"

Standing, I paced to the window and back then

doubled the trip. "Crap. If I knew, do you think I'd be wasting my time and money here?"

"Why *did* you come?"

"I thought you could tell me—"

She waggled her finger. "Uh, uh. You wanted to be told what to do. Then if my advice didn't work, it wouldn't be your fault." She straightened. "No, you must take responsibility to heal your timeline and move into the future."

"What do you suggest?"

She placed her hand over her chest. "Consult your heart. There is no other way."

"Can't you give me direction?"

She studied my face for a long moment before speaking. "You fear your brother in one life killed your then lover. Or worse, that you betrayed him."

My pulse picked up. Yes, she was right. I did fear Genevieve had contributed to Sheriff Adam's death. Although I remained uneasy with the eerie connection, my inner conviction knew Genevieve is/was me.

"Watch now, for answers," she said.

I sat quietly as images of Adrian and myself in our many guises swamped me like one of those morphing programs set on high speed. Egyptian faces blended with Greek or maybe Roman, moving to Celtic then Incan. One face became another, passing into too many to identify or track. Genders blended. I saw betrayal sometimes, expressions of hatred and love. As the past/present/future spun out, one thing became clear. I was linked to all these people. We were one being.

How had she pulled off the special effects?

"Gabriella, you don't need a deep comprehension of physics to understand basic facts. Why are you reluctant to allow Adrian a place in this lifetime?"

"He left Genevieve."

"Abandonment is one of the top fears all people share. Now, why do you think you sent Adrian away?"

"She, I couldn't rely on him. Adam, Adrian made a promise he didn't keep." Not too difficult to understand why I didn't trust Adrian to follow through in this lifetime.

I'd already worked some of this out, but the pieces fell into place like a breaking window played in reverse motion.

"To heal the pivotal life, along with this current one, you must release your sense of abandonment and step into the breach. Your action is imperative. The sooner the better."

"What do I do next?"

"If you are seeking a step-by-step plan, you will not find it here." She crossed her arms and sat back. "Nor will your Guardian help you with these last steps. You must progress on your own."

"Sheesh. I don't know why I bother coming here for answers."

Madame L. smiled. "I can see you understand your path. You've done excellent work. Don't falter in the final moments. Besides, your true love waits. I've never known you to turn aside from your destiny before."

Huh? We'd known each other before? Or had she meant something more? And who or what was a Guardian?

She stood. "I have an appointment, so must ask you to leave. Thank you for coming." Turning, she disappeared through the curtain, her cat at her heels.

Once again, I placed my payment in a Carnival

glass bowl and shut the outside door firmly on my way out. This time, instead of whirling thoughts and a surfeit of anger, I had a plan to concoct. True love waited, indeed.

Chapter Seventeen

I pondered Madame L.'s words about listening to my heart and following what I heard. Meditation is not my forte, heck, I don't like sitting still with nothing to do longer than a minute. But I'd try anything for answers.

Returning home, I knocked on Chastity's door, hoping she'd sit with me. No answer.

I entered my apartment and nestled on the couch with Cyrano. The lotus position was a bit beyond me, so I sat with my feet flat on the floor, the thumb and forefinger of each hand pressed together. After ten deep breaths, my body relaxed as Chastity had promised.

A vision of myself as Genevieve filtered before my mind's eye. She wore dark clothes. Her eyes were puffy with dark circles beneath. As I wondered whether her appearance meant Adam had died, I saw the flowers in her hand. The tombstone she faced. "Adam Price, Beloved Sheriff."

Tears ran down my cheeks. I took three deep breaths to settle my sudden angst. Why had I received this vision? How could this information help me now? Was I destined to love—and lose—Adrian again?

Finally, I understood. Cause or blame didn't matter. Only the life I actively participated with counted. The stalling tactics had to stop.

My pulse increased as excitement welled. My feet

wanted to dance, but I had to get to Adrian, first. Along with glee, I felt my nerves kick up. I hoped I'd get a positive reaction from the man I now admitted loving, but until I'd apologized, I couldn't count on a thing. I hugged Cyrano, grabbed my keys and left. Five minutes later, I knocked on Adrian's door.

His mocha latte colored orbs widened when he answered the door. Gone was his normal short ponytail. His hair fanned outward as if he'd continually tunneled his fingers through his dark waves. A flannel shirt was buttoned wrong and he went barefoot, even though the day's temperature held a decided bite.

"Oh. Hi. What brings you here?"

An entire case of beer could have been iced with his cool tone, but I refused to back down. "You. I'm here to see you. Mind if I come in, or do you want your neighbor across the hall to join in our conversation?"

The apartment door I'd noticed ajar shut abruptly.

Adrian moved aside.

I walked in, torn between the need to check out his apartment or speak about the meat of my mission. Glancing around quickly, I noted his computer set-up dominated a large portion of his living room. He had a flat screen television but not a jumbo-sized one. Piles of books and magazines were stacked next to comfortable chairs and on the coffee table. Big windows welcomed sunshine, which brought light and cheer to the space.

Ending my fast scan, I turned and faced him. He'd closed the door and leaned against the wood, watching me with a wary expression. My nerve endings jittered. I cleared my throat and clasped my hands together.

I knew my insecurities had caused me to push him away. Now I hoped to overcome my weaknesses. "I'm here to apologize."

"Apology accepted. That all? Because I have a project due this afternoon."

My ego urged me to stomp out, but I listened to my heart instead. "You were right. About us. Life is too short to waste living, how did you say it? In a "quagmire of fear?" Yeah, sounds right."

"Nice. Using my words in your apology."

I inhaled through my nose and held my temper. "I've been thinking. Remember? I asked for a bit of time? Well, I realized you were right. About everything."

"Thanks for letting me know." He reached for the doorknob.

My courage flagged at his lack of expression. I'd have to work for his every concession, and fast, before he threw me out.

"The dream, the one we shared, scared the crap out of me."

His hand dropped to his side. "Why? Dreams are the unconscious working out problems. Regardless of what Chastity believes about parallel lives, I think the similar dreams were more a fluke than anything."

I wouldn't argue over something I really couldn't explain. Not when the lesson I'd learned was more important than the way it had been delivered.

"Look, I'm trying...my problem is with trusting people not to leave me. Family members, close friends, the few lovers I've had. They've all left me behind. I figured they left because I wasn't worth their effort, didn't merit their attention. After time, I didn't trust my heart with anyone. I've learned most people have a fear of abandonment, but knowing other people are as afraid as me doesn't make my sense of loss any easier.

"I see."

"After the mind-blowing sex—"

"Mind-blowing?" He smiled.

I nodded. "Stellar. Anyway, first our remarkable physical connection, then the dream, then you asking me to live with you, well, those things combined sent me over the edge emotionally." I exhaled, shaking my head. "No excuse but I felt overloaded."

He rubbed his chin. "I see."

"Yeah, so, once I calmed down, I saw your words about fear were on target. I'm facing my mistakes." I took a deep breath. "Once again, I'm sorry. For not accepting the gift you offered. Most of all, for hurting your feelings."

He moved toward me. I couldn't read his expression.

"Why should I believe you? You've admitted to some heavy-duty anxiety. We haven't been apart even a full day. Most folks need counseling to find the insights you're spouting. Maybe you've exchanged fears. You know, admit to one hoping the other will disappear."

I clasped my shaking hands behind my back. No need to show him my weakness. Whoa. Exactly why I'd come. My hands fell to my sides. Let him think what he would.

"I could be, yeah. I'm new at all this self-realization stuff, but my apology is real. Now I've made my confession, I'll get out of your hair."

He held up a hand, palm out. "Not so fast."

My anger stirred. "I came to say I was sorry, not grovel."

His eyes shone. A smile tugged at his lips. "That's

better. I wondered what you'd done with the real Gabriella."

"What do you mean?"

"The woman I've come to know is savvy, funny, and loyal. She's got a core of strength most people don't see and, I suspect, she doesn't admit to having." He moved closer. "She's learning fear needn't rule her life." He stood before me. "She's got courage." His hands rested on my shoulders. "A gorgeous woman inside and out, and she would never, ever, grovel."

"Oh." Criminy, had he really called me gorgeous? And more importantly, courageous? My muscles relaxed a smidgen. I began hoping we could get back on track.

"It's my turn to apologize. I'd been attracted by your independence then got ticked off when you didn't want to let me lead." He pushed a lock of hair off my forehead. "A woman who's taken care of herself for years wouldn't jump at any man's offer to take over, but all I saw was you, not wanting me."

"Not totally true." I gulped. "I do want you."

"And I want you. On your terms, not mine," he said. "I've done some thinking, too."

I put my arms around his waist. "First, I appreciate you wanting to take care of me." I went up on my toes and kissed him on the lips. "It's a bit soon to move in with you, but thanks for the offer."

"My offer includes stellar sex as often as you want, dinners out unless you really want to cook, and a window crate for Cyrano's enjoyment."

"Hmm. You didn't mention cleaning. Are you a neat freak or a slob? These are important questions needing answers."

He ran his hands down my back. "I'll even put the toilet seat down for you."

"I may faint." I pulled his head down for a deep kiss. "You're making it difficult to pass up the new living arrangement, but I do need time."

"Take all the time you need." He halted, his lips poised over mine. "While you're thinking it over, I'll use my powers of persuasion. If they can't sway you, I'll practice."

I shivered with anticipation. "So I'm your training dummy?"

His steady regard calmed me. "You're no dummy, and I can use the rehearsal."

I cleared my throat. "Speaking of training, does your job offer stand?"

His steady regard calmed me. "You bet." He leaned back on his heels. "I thought you had doubts about starting your own business?"

"I do, but there have been developments. I got fired today." I held up my hand, palm out. "That's not why I apologized. I have enough money to live so I'm not only here because I need a job."

He regarded me for a long moment and nodded. "Okay."

"I'm not quite ready to start my business, so this is a stop gap measure while I look for something full-time. I thought you should know upfront."

"Fine. Mike and I will take whatever help you can give."

"Donna thinks there may be changes at J&J, but I'm not holding my breath."

"We'll deal with what comes, okay?"

"Okay." Phew. So far, so good. "Meanwhile, we do

have a link. One far deeper than I understand." I caught his gaze. "But even though I can't explain what you've already pointed out I can admit you're right. And I'd like to explore the connection with you. Wherever it leads."

His pupils darkened. "You're sure."

"Yes. Maybe I'll wimp out sometimes, but I know you'll hold my feet to the fire when necessary. So I'm asking—help me grow, please?"

"As long as you'll return the favor?"

I nodded.

"Then we've got a deal." He grinned. "We could shake hands or—"

"Seal our pact with a more vigorous physical expression." My forehead wrinkled. "Or do we have make-up sex first, then move on to shaking hands?"

He planted an open-mouthed kiss on my neck. "I vote for both. We shouldn't limit ourselves too soon. Doesn't bode well for the future."

"I like a flexible man."

"I'll show you flexible," he growled. "I have a king-sized bed right down the hall."

"By all means, let's give it a test drive."

He palm slapped his forehead. "After a short delay." Turning pleading eyes my way he said, "I'm out of condoms. Be right back. Will you wait?"

"I'll idle my engine until you get back."

He hadn't been gone five minutes when my phone dinged with a text from Chastity. "Where R U?"

As I typed in my response, the doorbell chimed. Adrian hadn't been kidding about "being right back." He could give The Flash lessons. Figuring he'd forgotten his key in his mad drugstore dash, I threw open the door.

"That test drive—"

Chastity and Mike stood before me. The test drive had to wait.

****

Adrian and Mike were sipping beer and lounging on his balcony. Chastity had pulled me aside with the excuse of "girl talk," and we were ensconced on the couch.

"Chastity, I went to see Madame L. and she made an odd comment. She said I'd have to take the final steps myself without help."

"Really? Huh."

"Yeah, and I began thinking about how you always had answers when I couldn't figure out what was happening."

She looked relieved. "No big deal. You know I read a lot."

"But when I faced my lowest point, you didn't answer your door when I knocked."

She flinched.

"Up until then, you'd always been there when I needed you. Kind of like an advisor. A counselor. Or maybe, a *guardian*."

She jumped to her feet. "I could use more wine. How about you?"

"You've got half a glass."

She checked her wine level and sank back into her chair.

I leaned forward. "Can you tell me what's going on? Sometimes I had the feeling you knew what was happening before I told you."

She nodded. "Sometimes I did. I can't explain

everything, but I can say I was assigned as your Guardian."

"Are you human or some kind of ET?"

"Human! Well, most humans are from other planets originally, but that's a long story, and I get the feeling you'd rather know how I came to be in your life."

"You guessed correctly."

"Perhaps the easiest way to understand my work is to tell you there are humans who can operate on more than one plane at a time. They work as Destiny Guardians, cosmic guides you could say."

"So you moved next door and became my friend because it was your job?" Shoot. I thought I'd moved past the needy stage. Guess not.

"No, don't let the paranoia grab you. I became your friend because you are a wonderful person. Guardians are trained to remain objective, but I couldn't with you. Keeping my assignment a secret bothered me. I'm glad we can talk it out now, and I hope you'll want to remain friends."

"Can you tell me about your assignment? Why me? I'm not special."

"You're wrong, so wrong." She brushed her hair back from her face. "Every person is important to the universe as a whole, but sometimes one person can generate a far-reaching change through healing a pivotal timeline."

"Madame LaMere mentioned that the first time I saw her." I snapped my fingers. "Wait a minute. She's a Guardian, too, isn't she?" I saw a third face. "And Leonard. Is he one of you?"

"Madame L. is a Destiny Sentinel, with a different

set of responsibilities and abilities. Leonard, yes, he's a Guardian." She sipped her wine. "You were considered at risk due to Joel's influence. A possibility existed you would not meet Adrian in this lifetime. Or, if you did meet, possibly not allow him close. This would tip the scales in the wrong direction."

I had a feeling I didn't want to know what her last comment meant. "Um, did I do okay? In the mission department? I didn't cause you to get a demotion or something, did I?

"You're an ace, and given we're here and the vibe between you and Adrian is smoking hot, I'd say you don't have a thing to worry about."

"Can you tell me how my actions affect the whole?"

Her forehead wrinkled. "I'm afraid I can't, not without endangering potential results. But you shouldn't worry. The future is on track thanks to your taking a chance on Adrian this afternoon. Agreeing to work together for mutual growth has made a huge difference."

"What if we screw up? Split apart down the line?"

"Doesn't matter. Your timeline healing is complete."

"So why don't I feel different?"

She shrugged. "Not my department." Grinning, she said, "Stop worrying. Ya done good."

"You realize this is all too weird, right?"

"Do you want me to wipe out your memory? No? Then let's join the guys."

I knew I'd have plenty more questions once I had time to think. For the moment, I wanted nothing more than to snuggle with my new guy. Once again reading my mind, Chastity hustled Mike out the door, leaving Adrian and myself alone.

I knew just how to handle the solitude.

Chapter Eighteen

"Getting late. Are you hungry?" Adrian pulled open the refrigerator door. "I think I could toss a meal together, unless you want to go out?"

"I'm more interested in learning whether your drug store trip was successful."

His eyes glittered. "Two value packs. Think fifty will be enough?"

"I love a man who not only plans ahead, but knows how to save money. We should be okay for a couple of days, right?"

His gaze dropped to my lips. "I love a woman who thinks big."

Heat rapidly spread through my body, and he hadn't laid a finger on me. "Are you digging for a compliment? Did I forget to tell you how much I enjoyed you last time? Shame on me."

He moved to my side quicker than a streaking comet and laid his lips against my cheek. "Why are we talking?"

He kissed my neck, moving slowly to my jaw line.

My breath came faster.

Grazing my ear with his lips, he flicked his tongue against my ear lobe. Damn. Jelly knees again. I hoped we'd be moving to the couch or his promised king-sized bed soon.

We kissed, our tongues tangled and explored. He

pulled away, drawing my bottom lip between his teeth as he withdrew. I was pleased both of us breathed in little shallow pants.

"You did promise me a tour and a test drive," I managed.

He smoothed the hair back from my forehead. "I did. Are you sure?"

My lungs couldn't catch air, so I nodded.

Placing his hand at the small of my back, he ushered me down the hall. I'd never understood how the gesture could seduce, but the warmth of his hand settled yet excited me.

His bedroom was large but not so big you needed to take rations on your way to the bathroom. The king-sized bed looked in proportion to the room, and was covered with a typically masculine color combination of dark blues and ivory. I was surprised a small seating area with a stack of books was more dominant than the flat screen television. More books were stacked on a nightstand. The door to a walk-in closet stood ajar, but I couldn't see inside. Given I'd usually seen him clad in T-shirts and jeans, I expected he had more room than he needed.

"Like what you see?"

"Looks like a bachelor pad."

He opened his mouth, but shut it without speaking. Instead, he laid a kiss on me. His fingers fumbled at my buttons. "Shit. Mr. Suave and debonair I'm not."

I placed my forefinger over his lips. "No. We will not run ourselves down."

His palms cupped my face. "You're right." He nipped then laved my lower lip. "No expectations, no stress."

We took our time undressing each other, stopping to admire and caress the nearly naked views along the way. Hand in hand, we slipped onto the bed, me on my back, Adrian propped on his side.

"Come here, big boy." I pulled his head to mine, covering his lips with mine. I dimly noted our combined heat and the triggered air conditioning.

He smoothed one hand over my jaw and neck, his touch gentle, light. His butterfly kisses simultaneously excited but didn't demand.

I drifted in a haze of tenderness, a feeling unlike any I'd had with any other lover. He moved over me, supporting his weight with his arms, and a sense of quiet urgency infected us. Still, the energy surrounding us remained almost peaceful or maybe content was a better word. As if we knew and accepted we belonged together and had stopped fighting the attraction. I knew I had come to terms with past, present, and future, and Adrian's part in my lives.

When he finally entered me, we moved in slow accord. Floating beneath him, I let my anger and doubt go, trusting in the promise of us. Our momentum built moment by moment.

"Open your eyes, Gabriella."

I did and fell into his dark gaze.

"Feel us. Sense what we have together."

I laced my fingers with his.

"I adore you. Worship you. Give you my all."

I didn't need time to think. Nor did I fear speaking. "And I you."

Untold moments later, we came together. A white light filled with golden flakes enhanced the room. I opened my senses to a cosmic orgasm engulfed us, moving outward to encompass the apartment, then Harteville, the country, the world.

Chastity was right. One or two people could change the world with love.

****

A text came the next morning as I lay beside Adrian, his arm and leg thrown over mine. I took a moment to admire the tan skin and fine hair on his muscular calf then grabbed my phone from the nightstand. My stomach clenched when I saw Donna had left a message saying "NEWS. CALL ME."

Easing out from under the still sleeping Adrian, I used speed dial while searching his kitchen for coffee.

"You won't believe what's happened," she said in lieu of "hello." "I don't believe it and I was in the meeting."

"Tell me before I pee my pants." I looked down, conscious I wore no pants. Or clothes.

"Howie is gone."

"Gone?"

"Finito. Out on his ass. Probably in the bar closest to work, licking his wounds. Do taverns open this early? Never mind. I like the picture I painted and don't need truth."

"Girlfriend, you are shitting me."

"I printed out your reports and gave them to Malachi. You should have seen him turn red, especially after he got a look at the Internet usage log Carma compiled."

Had I not been so mellow after a night of hot sex, I'd have been jealous at not being in the meeting.

She inhaled noisily. "He asked if I thought you'd come back. You will, won't you? They want to promote you to senior analyst."

"No thanks. They'll probably hire a relative to run the department."

"Another bit of news." Her voice rose at the end. "I've been made manager. You'll be reporting to me, and I'll make sure you get the salary and ongoing raises you deserve."

We squealed together then I returned Earthside. "Donna, you know I love you like a sister and working for you is a dream, but I can't."

"What? Why not? Don't worry about hurting our friendship. I know we can be professional. We fight, we work stuff out, we have a drink together."

"Not the problem." I hesitated, unsure how to continue, then decided to bare my heart. "Remember I told you about the new man I was interested in, Adrian?"

"Yeah, baby. Sounds like a winner."

"He is, and he's asked me to work for him and his partner. They want me to manage their office. This is an opportunity I can't pass up."

"I hear a "but" in your answer."

"But, I don't know if there's really enough work, or if I should combine business with pleasure." I kept my voice at a murmur, hoping Adrian didn't hear my reluctance.

"I'll hold the job for you until you tell me you don't want to work for J&J." She snorted. "Did you really think I'd toss you over? Get real, girl, and pull your confidence out of your butt. You won't go anywhere with a mealy mouth."

I laughed. "You're right. Wish me luck?"

"Confident women don't need luck. Just brains.

Make your moves. I have total faith in you." She cleared her throat. "If your plan bombs, give me a call. Failure doesn't mean you didn't do your best. Maybe the guy is an ass, someone who doesn't deserve you."

Ending the call, I turned. Adrian stood in the doorway. "You don't have to work for us if you have something better," he said.

Although his expression was clear, I heard the slight hitch indicating he wasn't sure what more to say. He moved into the kitchen and pulled out the coffee I hadn't found earlier.

I told him about Howie's demise and the offered promotion. "So, I hate leaving Donna in the lurch. But, I made you a promise I don't want to break."

"I'll help you however I can."

The tone of his voice, along with a loving gaze persuaded me he meant every word.

"Whatever hours you can give us will be better than the way Mike and I are limping along. You're what our paperwork needs." He kissed the sensitive spot behind my ear. "You're what *I* need. In every way."

"Those sentiments go both ways," I said.

He pulled me into his embrace. "Should I make coffee or can I interest you in a king-sized bed needing more christening?"

I drew his lips to mine. Some questions don't need answers.

****

One month later, Cyrano and I moved in with Adrian. Life's too damn short, ya know? Adrian didn't take my half of the expenses. He said my home-cooked meals were so good he got the better deal. I didn't admit to ordering out from Mancini's several times a week, and he didn't blow my cover. What a guy. Really, why had I ever put him off?

I had no problem handling both my new job at J&J and working on Adrian and Mike's business records. Donna was a joy to work for and Adrian was more organized than he'd let on. I still held my vision of financing creative folks, and socked away my half of living expenses plus more toward that end. My goal would be recognized, sooner than later.

Speaking of dreams, I still walked in other worlds, sometimes accompanied by Adrian, but more often alone. Chastity and Leonard gave me pointers and I'd learned how to choose a probability to anchor myself to while working on healing the bits and pieces floating in and out of my consciousness.

Chastity and Mike are so tight they squeak. He knows about her Guardian work and thinks it's cool.

Madame L. tells me I may be making a trip, soon. I'm not sure I want to know more.

There's only so much a girl can take, ya know?